S0-AXR-017

Property of Koeningsmaul
Middle School Library

Can I Get There
by Candlelight?

6714
F
Dot

JEAN SLAUGHTER DOTY

Can I Get There by Candlelight?

ILLUSTRATED BY TED LEWIN

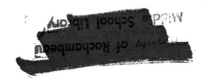

Middle School Library
Property of Rochambeau

Macmillan Publishing Co., Inc.
New York
Collier Macmillan Publishers
London

Copyright © 1980 Jean Slaughter Doty
Copyright © 1980 Macmillan Publishing Co., Inc.
All rights reserved. No part of this book may be reproduced
or transmitted in any form or by any means, electronic or
mechanical, including photocopying, recording or by any
information storage and retrieval system, without
permission in writing from the Publisher.

Macmillan Publishing Co., Inc.
866 Third Avenue, New York, N.Y. 10022
Collier Macmillan Canada, Ltd.
Printed in the United States of America

10   9   8   7   6   5   4   3   2   1

LIBRARY OF CONGRESS CATALOGING IN PUBLICATION DATA

Doty, Jean Slaughter, date
Can I get there by candlelight?
SUMMARY: Young Gail Simmons and her pony befriend
a girl from another century.
[1. Space and time—Fiction. 2. Ponies—Fiction]
I. Lewin, Ted. II. Title.
PZ7.D7378Can   [Fic]   79-24466   ISBN 0-02-732670-5

To
Patricia Bonsall Stuart
—for a number of shared happy reasons.

How many miles to Babylon?
Three score miles and ten.
Can I get there by candlelight?
Yes, and back again.
If your heels are nimble and light,
You can get there by candlelight.

—Mother Goose

Can I Get There by Candlelight?

Chapter One

The small room at the top of the old carriage house was hot and airless. But I loved the smell and the clutter of forgotten things, and Prudence, my gray and white striped cat, liked to come up here with me. She sat on the curved top of the small trunk near the window, watching a fly that buzzed against the dusty glass.

I sat on the trunk beside her for a minute. If I pressed my left shoulder against the frame of the round window, and ignored the cobwebs that tangled in my hair, I could just see the paddock where Candy, my gray Welsh pony, grazed in the morning sunlight.

"Move, Pru." I lifted the purring cat and put her down on the floor. "I want to see what's in the trunk." Pru narrowed her yellow eyes, fluffed out her long coat with a quick shake, and curled her tail around her paws as I knelt beside her on the dusty floor.

I pulled the trunk around to face the light from

the window. The leather covering was split and peeling, and the brass latch was dark with age. I could barely see a faintly traced pattern of leaves and flowers on the plate around the latch and indistinct markings which might be initials, though I couldn't be sure.

It took me several minutes, but finally I felt a short catch on one side. When I pressed it the oval latch sprang open, and I lifted the curved trunk lid gently.

From a thick nest of dry tissue paper I lifted a strangely shaped saddle. It took me a few moments of puzzled inspection before I realized that it was a small sidesaddle, with two curved horns, and a single stirrup leather which was dry and cracked. I'd seen pictures of sidesaddles before, but I'd never seen a real one.

"Wouldn't it be fun to learn how to ride sidesaddle, Pru?" I said to the cat beside me. I'd always wanted to try. I'd even gone so far as to bump around on Candy, sitting sideways in her regular saddle, but that hadn't worked at all well and I'd given it up.

I put the saddle down, very gently, beside Pru, and pushed my long hair away from my face. I took another layer of yellowing paper from the trunk and then lifted out an armful of dark green fabric. I unfolded it carefully, draping it over the graceful horns of the saddle. There was a jacket and a wide, long matching skirt—a sidesaddle habit for a young girl.

The last thing at the bottom of the trunk was a round black and green striped box fastened with a black braided cord. Inside the box, in a crumpled hollow of pale green tissue paper, was a small dark green felt hat. The brim was turned up on one side and a short red feather, its color still bright, was tucked into the band of faded ribbon.

"What a pretty thing," I said to Pru. I sat back on my heels. I'd opened all the other trunks and boxes up here, and looked at the faded paintings leaning against the wall, but for the first time since I had found this room in the old carriage house, I felt like an intruder.

I put everything back into the trunk as gently as I could, pressed the latch shut with a tiny click, and slid the trunk back to its original place by the window. I called softly to Pru and we felt our way down the shadowy stairs.

The main floor of the carriage house was dim and cool. The harness room and cleaning room and the huge carriage room echoed with emptiness. Only a broken two-wheeled pony cart was left, shoved into a far dark corner. It looked more like a skeleton than a pony cart. Its delicate sides curved unevenly as it leaned against the wall. On each side a small carriage lamp, tipped in its holder, was blurry with cobwebs. One of the wheels was cracked and a shaft was broken, and the paint was thick and dark with dust.

"Everything in here was sold at the auction last

summer," the real estate agent had told us when she'd pushed the heavy, warped doors open for my parents to look inside. "No one even knew there were carriages still here until the surveyors came through last spring. The main house and the stables have been gone for years.

"So there's nothing left now except this, and the coachman's house, and the shed in the field. And even they'll all be gone by early next winter. Hard to imagine that they'll be building condominiums here so soon, but I guess that's progress."

She'd backed out into the stone-paved courtyard. "Even that old wreck of a cart belongs to somebody. I don't know who, but they'd better come get it or it'll be scrapped along with everything else on the place."

She'd shut the door, brushing flaking paint from her hands, and we'd gone back to the small coachman's house my parents had just agreed to rent for the summer. We had to live somewhere until the builders finished our new house—it wouldn't be ready for us until September—and except for two miserably dark houses almost in the middle of town, this was the only house for rent in the area.

It was a long way from the center of town, but this didn't matter. There were orchards and woods and open fields around the house, and, most important of all, there was a place for me to keep Candy. The agent had called it a shed, but it was really a snug stone stable with a single stall, tucked in the corner of a grassy paddock. I'd already inspected it, while the agent and my parents talked about drains, and I knew it would be perfect.

Dad would be so busy traveling most of the summer that it wouldn't matter to him where we lived. Mom would be spending most of her time with the builders and architects and shopping for things for the new house. And I could think of the summer ahead, at last, with a quick shiver of delight. I would have Candy, and a nice place to keep her, and miles of woods and fields for us to explore together.

Chapter Two

Candy was waiting for me with her head over the paddock gate. I put her in the stall, gave her an apple, and got my grooming things. She stood patiently while I worked on her coat, and glowed like freshly polished silver when I finished by brushing her pale mane smooth.

The stable was bright and airy, with a wonderful smell of fresh shavings, sunlight, pony, and hay. It had probably been used to rest tired carriage horses, or to nurse sick ones safely away from the main stable, many years ago. There was just the one big box stall with a storage room beside it, which I'd filled with hay and bedding and grain.

Our moving from Minnesota had been unexpected and hectic—Dad had been transferred by his company with no more than a few weeks' warning. Suddenly the life I'd always known and taken for granted had vanished like a popped balloon. All my good friends, my school, and almost everything else that mattered to me had to be left behind. The one thing that made it all bearable was that Candy could come with me, and she'd arrived safely in an enormous transcontinental horse van two days after we'd moved into the rented coachman's house.

She'd been tired and stained and frightened and looked as bewildered as I'd felt when we'd moved. I fussed over her with hot soapy baths and slow walks in the sun. Caring for her and settling her in helped me push the confusion of the past few weeks from my mind, and I refused to think of the grim gray autumn ahead. New school, new teachers, and the nervous effort of trying to make new friends—I'd face that when the time came. But in the meantime, Candy and I had the short, golden summer to share.

I put Candy's bridle on and led her out of the stall. With true Welsh pony spirit she'd bounded right back from her weary trip. After a few days of rest she was bright and fresh, and as eager as I was to go out into the fields and woods around us. I took her through the paddock gate and wiggled onto her bare back, and we rode into the apple orchard that stretched out beyond the paddock fence.

Candy let out a buck and a kick of pleasure as we reached the top of the orchard hill. I loosened the reins and she went off into a gallop, her unshod hoofs swishing through the tall orchard grass. The breeze blew against my face and lifted my hair as we circled through the tangled old trees, jumping fallen branches until both of us were finally content to slow down to a walk and catch our breaths.

I rode Candy over to the towering stone wall that ran the whole length of the orchard. High as I was on Candy's back, I still couldn't see over the top of the wall—nothing but the heavy tops of thick trees on the other side. The breeze had died, and the sun was getting hot in the orchard. It would be nice to be able to ride in the woods for a while, if I could only find a way through the wall.

Where the ground dipped into a hollow we found a narrow iron gate, almost hidden behind a riot of overgrown honeysuckle and ivy. I shortened my reins, slid off Candy's back, and led her over to the gate. It was a thin pattern of iron set in a narrow archway of stone. Delicate designs of flowers were woven into the upright bars that were topped with spiky iron leaves.

I pulled some of the honeysuckle away from the latch and the hinges. I tried to jiggle the latch, which was patchy with rust, then braced myself and tugged at the gate as hard as I could. It moved a little, but then it jammed again. I took a step back and looked at it thoughtfully.

On the far side of the gate, traces of a narrow path led invitingly into the shade of the woods. But there was no question of jumping Candy over the gate, not

with those menacing, sharp-edged iron leaves on the top and the curved stone archway above.

Candy snatched a mouthful of sweet orchard grass and dribbled friendly green bubbles down the side of my blue sleeveless shirt. I pushed her head away absently and rubbed her between her ears—there had to be *some* way to get through the gate.

I picked up a stone near the wall and tapped the latch gently. The stone left bright marks on the metal, but nothing moved. I hesitated—after all, it wasn't my gate, and I didn't want to damage it—but every minute the sun was getting hotter, and the flies were beginning to collect around Candy. With more determination I banged the stone against the latch. There was a thump, and a click, and the latch slid open.

I knelt and yanked at the honeysuckle vines. A few sleepy bees bumbled out of the yellow and white flowers and the fragrance of the honeysuckle mixed with the rich smell of the loam around the roots of the vines. I picked a honeysuckle flower, bit off the end, and sipped the thin, sweet nectar as I went on tugging at the stubborn vines.

I was stubborn, too. I wanted to get into the cool shade of the woods. I stood up, brushed the loam from my knees, and gave the gate an angry kick. With a shriek of metal that gave me goosebumps and set Candy dancing at the end of the reins, the narrow gate swung open.

Hot and sweaty and proud of myself, I led Candy through the narrow opening and jumped up on her back. The welcoming woods were so deep in shadow that the sunlight shimmered as though we were going underwater.

I straightened the reins, pressed my heels against Candy's sides, and started along the mossy path that curved through the shadows ahead.

Chapter Three

The path was soft and springy and Candy's hoofs made no sound as we moved deeper into the woods. The ground dipped; ferns and soft-leaved vines tumbled along the edges of the path. When we came to a stream, Candy walked carefully through the bright water, stopping to ruffle the ripples with her muzzle, and scrambled up the slope on the far side.

The path widened. Candy broke into a soft jog and then into a gentle canter. Her head was up and her ears were pricked. Cool and contented, I rode on a loose rein as we cantered almost dreamily through the dim and shaded woods.

The path made an abrupt turn and came to an end at the edge of a wide, sunlit lawn. A tiny white dog, barking hysterically, came bouncing across the grass toward us. Startled, Candy flung her head in the air and whirled violently to one side and I went sailing right over her shoulder, landing with a *whomp* on the lawn.

I sat up quickly, furious at myself for falling off, and at Candy for having shied so wildly, and at the noisy little dog that had taken us by surprise. "Shut up, you silly thing," I said crossly to the dog, which was jumping up and down beside me, still barking.

At the sound of my voice it did stop barking, and jumped onto my lap with a flurry of soft white fur. It started to try to lick my face, and what with my hair tumbled over my eyes and the busy little dog, it was several breathless moments before I could find Candy.

She hadn't gone far. She was standing just at the edge of the woods, with one ear cocked toward me and the other toward the bright grass of the lawn. And I saw dizzily that she wasn't wearing her bridle.

The darned thing was lying on the path between us in a heap of twisted leather. I must have grabbed at Candy's mane as I started to go off, caught the back of the bridle instead, and pushed it right over her ears as I fell.

"Whoa, Candy," I said, trying to make my voice sound sweet and calm. I pushed the dog away gently and then grabbed it again—I was afraid it might rush over to bark at Candy. The pony looked at me with her big dark eyes sparkling. I knew that look of hers and my heart sank. Candy knew very well she was now free to do just as she pleased, and she was busily weighing all the choices she had.

How far had we come? I couldn't begin to guess. I

only knew home seemed suddenly very far away, on the other side of thick woods which seemed endlessly deep and dark now that I was no longer on Candy.

"Whoa, Candy," I said again. I patted the little dog cautiously. It was quiet in my arms, watching me with merry dark eyes and wagging the curled plume of its tail. Holding it carefully with one hand, I fumbled with my belt buckle, pulling the belt out of the loops of my jeans, and slipped it over the dog's white ruff as a makeshift leash.

I searched in my pockets but I'd forgotten to bring any sugar. I tried to pretend I had some, anyway. Very slowly I got to my feet, picked up the bridle, and hid it behind my back. With the bridle and the end of my belt in one hand, and the other hand outstretched as though I was holding a lump of sugar, I moved toward Candy.

It almost worked—she almost let me catch her. But at the very last second, just as my fingers brushed her shoulder, she gave a wicked toss of her pretty head, made a dive to one side, and set sail at a gallop across the open lawn. Standing at the dark edge of the woods, with the little dog barking wildly again beside me, I watched Candy carry her silvery tail like a banner as she swept across the lawn and out of sight.

Chapter Four

I sighed miserably, tried to shake some of the tangles out of the bridle, and set out across the lawn to follow Candy. The little white dog danced beside me.

It started to bark again and bounced in a circle. I turned and saw a dark-haired girl, dressed in what seemed to be a long white nightgown, running across the lawn toward us.

I felt my face grow so hot that my cheeks stung. There are few things in the world that can make a rider feel more foolish than to stand and watch a rider-less pony running off as free as a bird. That was bad enough, but now I'd been caught trespassing as well, my pony was playing hide-and-seek somewhere out of sight on the beautiful lawn, and I was holding some-one's dog a prisoner.

I knelt quickly and freed the dog. It raced over to the girl, jumping happily up against her full skirts, and ran in circles around her, still barking, as she came near.

"Hello, are you hurt?" she said to me anxiously. "Oh, hush, Nanette." Her voice was soft, but the dog stopped barking. She leaned over and scooped it up in her arms.

"There, that's better." She looked at me questioningly. "Are you hurt?" she asked again. "I'm so sorry my dog frightened your pony. Is there anything I can do?"

I was frantic and breathless and I just stood there with my toes curling in my tattered sneakers. The pretty girl with gray eyes, her wavy hair caught back from her face with a wide blue ribbon, was not wearing a nightgown at all. She was wearing a pale dress with a delicate pattern of blue flowers and the dress was tied with a matching blue sash. The shoes that showed under the folds of her skirt were narrow and black and buttoned high above her ankles.

"Thank you. No. I'm fine," I finally managed to say. "I'm sorry to be bothering you like this. I'm sorry my pony is running around on your lawn. . . ."

I stopped awkwardly and took a quick breath. "My name is Gail," I said. "Gail Simmons. I live over there—" I gestured vaguely in the direction of the woods. While I struggled to be polite, my mind was full of visions of Candy racing away for endless miles in country that was completely strange to her, and to me. I was beginning to panic. I could puzzle out later why this girl was wearing such funny clothes, but just now, all I could think of was trying to find and catch Candy.

"I'm Hilary Blake," the girl said gravely. "How do you do. Come, let's look for your pony together. I'd love to help." She put the dog down on the soft green lawn. "Be good, Nanette," she said firmly. "Don't frighten the pony again."

We walked quickly across the smooth grass. "I was there," said Hilary, waving one hand toward a little white summerhouse over to our right. I'd been too frantic to notice it before. It was open on all sides and crisscrossed with latticework so that it looked almost like snowy lace. "I'm embroidering a pillow for Mother's birthday, but I really hate needlework. I'm sorry you were thrown, but as long as you're all right—you are, really? Are you sure? It's nice to have company. . . ."

We reached the top of a gentle rise in the lawn. The far side sloped down to the shore of a lake. Two long gardens, edged with tall crisp hedges and massed with beds of pink roses, curved back toward the summerhouse. In the center of the oval lawn between the gardens Candy, looking like a marble lawn decoration, stood watching a pair of swans on the lake.

We stopped. "I think she's one of the prettiest ponies I've ever seen," said Hilary. Candy did look nice. Her pale gray dapples shone and her silver mane and tail shimmered in the faint breeze that came from the lake. But I was in no mood to admire Candy's finer points—I knew what was going on in that pony mind of hers, behind her sweet expression.

"She is," I said tensely, "sometimes a little hard to catch."

This was an out-and-out lie. Candy was *awful* to catch. Raised on a farm where the ponies ran free in enormous fields, she'd been half wild when I'd first gotten her as a three-year-old. And though she'd been easy to break and was generally kind and good, sudden freedom went to her head like too much grain on a rainy day. She simply was not going to let herself be caught until *she* decided she was ready.

Candy turned her head toward us, pricked her neat little ears, and blew softly through flared nostrils. I stretched my hand toward her, thinking positive thoughts about apples and carrots and sugar, but Candy wasn't fooled. She always knew when I was just pretending and really had nothing for her.

She took one step toward us. "There," said Hilary in her soft voice. "She's going to be good."

But Candy had no intention of being good. With a toss of her pretty head and a flick of her tail, she spun away from us. In two galloping strides she had jumped into the rose garden, set herself neatly, and jumped the tall hedge at the back. She gave a buck and a kick and vanished.

"She *is* a good jumper, isn't she!" Hilary said admiringly.

I groaned out loud. Now, on top of everything else, there were deep hoofprints in the soft bed of the rose garden. "I'm so sorry," I said feebly. "I'll come right

19

back and fix those, just as soon as I've caught Candy—"

Hilary shook her head. "Please don't worry about it," she said. "The gardeners will take care of it."

I gave Hilary a frantic look. I could just imagine what my parents would have said if they'd found galloping hoofprints through their flower beds.

"There are some teacakes in the summerhouse," Hilary said. "Let's go back and get some—do you think she'd like them well enough to let us catch her?"

I didn't know what Candy might think of teacakes, but I'd often bribed her successfully with tollhouse cookies, so I thought Hilary's idea might work. I was ready to try anything. I said so, and we hurried back toward the summerhouse.

Candy had already discovered the teacakes, and she did like them. We found her standing with her front hoofs up on the white steps of the summerhouse, her head stretched inside as far as she could reach. There was the sound of a crash and Hilary giggled. "There goes the plate, I should imagine," she said cheerfully.

Hilary seemed to think it was funny, but I was furious. I tiptoed up to Candy's shoulder—she'd been too busy to see us coming—and looped the bridle reins around her neck.

Candy tried to jump away, but it was too late. Yanking grimly on the reins, I stopped her in her guilty tracks, and in a flash I had the bit in her mouth and the bridle behind her ears.

I buckled the throatlatch and collapsed onto the

Property of Rochambeau
Middle School Library

grass, my knees weak with relief. I held the reins so tightly that I could feel the little square buckle on the ends bite into my fingers. It was a comforting feeling —I'd had enough of Candy's independence.

Hilary smiled. I heard the sound of her narrow shoes tapping lightly as she went into the summerhouse and came back carrying a pitcher and a tall glass on a silver tray.

"You must be tired," she said sympathetically. "Would you like some lemonade?"

"Thank you." I took the frosty glass gratefully. The lemonade was bright and sweet—I'd never tasted anything so good. I tried not to be greedy, but I was terribly hot and thirsty, and the glass was soon empty.

With a whisk of her full skirt Hilary put the tray on the grass beside me. "Do have more," she said. "And here you are, Candy. I've brought you another cake."

Candy accepted the small pink cake with gentle good manners.

"I'm sorry I can't offer you one," said Hilary to me, "but Candy did push the plate off the tray, and all the cakes spilled on the floor."

I started to jump to my feet. "Let me go clean them up," I said quickly. Hoofprints in the rose garden, and goodness knows how much damage Candy'd done galloping all over the lawn, and now teacakes all over the summerhouse floor—and probably a broken plate, as well, from the sound of the crash we'd heard. What an embarrassing introduction to a new neighbor.

Chapter Five

Hilary put out a hand to stop me. "Please, don't worry about it. The maid will tidy everything when she comes down for the tray later."

She sat down beside me on the lawn, spreading her skirts in a wide circle. She clasped her hands in her lap and leaned forward eagerly. "Tell me," she said. "Do you live close by? Or in the village?"

"I don't really know," I said, feeling slightly stupid. "Candy and I followed the path through the woods and I don't know how far we came. We're new here. My parents have just rented a house for the summer—"

Hilary gave a quick nod. "This is our summer place, too." I looked up over her shoulder and I could just make out the top of a long roofline, with several chimneys and two wings, almost hidden by a row of enormous trees which curved away from the house to edge the sweep of a long drive.

"We live in the city in the winter," said Hilary, "and spend the summer in our house out here. But just now my parents are in Europe with my older brother, Hugh. I wanted to go with them so badly, but I had influenza most of last winter, and the doctor said traveling would be too tiring for me this summer." Hilary made a face. "So I'm practically a prisoner out here for the summer, with nobody but a new governess to keep me company. She thinks just about everything I want to do is either unladylike or too exhausting for me. And teaches me French verbs every chance she gets."

Hilary sighed. Nanette, who'd been in the summer-house licking up crumbs, trotted down the steps and cuddled close to Hilary's side. "But at least Madame lets me alone when I come down to the summerhouse in the afternoons. She says the sunlight here gives her headaches, and will spoil her complexion."

Hilary shook her head. "I think she's homesick for Switzerland, and I have a terrible feeling she's planning with my mother to have me go there to boarding school next winter." She was silent for a moment, stroking Nanette's head with her hand.

She looked up with a smile. "That's enough about me. Tell me about yourself. Do you always ride like that? Bareback, without a saddle? Did you come here from the West, and are those the kind of trousers the cowboys wear?"

Startled, I looked down at my ragged jeans which were bleached and faded and nicely frayed at the bottom.

"Sort of," I said.

"It's just that I've never seen a girl ride astride before," said Hilary. "Though I know it's done, of course," she added hastily.

I half-closed my eyes and looked at her uncertainly through my lashes. I felt my head beginning to spin. I'd had a long day, I was hot and tired, and I couldn't seem to make much sense out of what Hilary was saying.

"I think," I said slowly, "I'd better start home."

Hilary looked crushed. "I wish you wouldn't go so soon," she said. "I've really enjoyed meeting you and helping you catch your pony. Will you and Candy come again when you can stay longer?"

"Of course," I said. I hesitated for just a second. "I mean, I'll come if I possibly can."

"Tomorrow." Hilary was insistent. She stood up and brushed a few clinging blades of grass from her skirts, putting her hand on Candy's bridle as I flung myself up on the pony's back and gathered the reins. She straightened the pony's forelock and tucked it under her browband. "Good-by, Candy," she said. She looked up at me. "Is Candy her whole name?"

"It's short for Candlelight," I said.

Hilary smiled. "Then you'll certainly be back," she said. "Remember the old nursery rhyme? 'How many miles to Babylon? Three score miles and ten—'"

I smiled back. "'Can I get there by candlelight? Yes, and back again.'"

"Exactly." Hilary let go of Candy's bridle.

With a quick wave I turned Candy and kicked her into a canter. I was too confused and tired to worry any more about hoofprints on the lawn. Candy reached for the bit and a fleck of foam flew from her muzzle.

"Good-by!" I heard Hilary's voice faintly over Candy's hoofbeats. I half turned to wave again and caught a final glimpse of Hilary standing next to the summerhouse, with her hand raised and her little white dog sitting silently by her feet.

Chapter Six

I wasn't exactly sure where the path entered the woods, but Candy remembered. We flew down the slope of the lawn and Candy turned and plunged into the woods, onto the dark path, without a moment's hesitation. I hung on for dear life, giving her her head, and it wasn't until I caught sight of the twinkle of the stream that I sat up and brought the pony back to a walk.

Candy was breathing hard and her neck was covered with sweat, so I wouldn't let her stop to drink as we splashed hurriedly through the shallow stream and trotted up the path on the other side.

I pulled Candy back to a walk again and gradually she and I both began to calm down. The woods were quiet. The late afternoon light was soft. Pale sunlight slanted mistily through the trees and made blurry shadows on the path.

I glanced at my watch. It was almost six. Mother would probably be searching for my broken body all through the apple orchard where I'd told her I'd be riding that afternoon. I felt harassed and guilty, but I knew if I hurried, Candy would be much too hot to put away. And I didn't want to explain where I'd been all afternoon—I wasn't sure I really knew how to explain Hilary, even to myself.

I sighed wearily, and patted Candy on her shoulder. Her head drooped—she was tired, too. Slowly we walked down the mossy path, and when the path made a last turn we were very glad to see the silhouette of the iron gate that led to the orchard, its graceful pattern of curved leaves showing sharply against the pale orchard grass behind it.

I slid off to the ground and led Candy through the gate, careful not to let her reins catch on the iron leaves. I shoved the gate shut behind us. It looked strangely bare without its tangled cover of vines, so I kicked a few dead leaves against it and hauled myself up again on the pony's back.

Candy toiled up the hill toward her paddock and I looked back at the gate. Evening shadows had reached it and it could barely be distinguished from the dark woods behind it.

"Maybe next time we should just stay in the orchard," I said out loud to Candy.

I made the pony comfortable in her stall just as quickly as I could and hurried guiltily up to the house.

"I'm sorry I'm late!" I shouted, and let the screen door slam behind me to announce I was home. But I was greeted only by the echo of the slam and a note propped against the sugar bowl on the kitchen table.

"Home later, meeting with the architect, sliced ham and cheese in refrigerator and some frozen dinners in freezer if you want something hot. Love, Mom."

I sagged into a chair by the table with a sigh of relief. I hadn't known how I would explain why I was late. I was tired, my leg was a little stiff from my fall, and, mostly, I was puzzled by Hilary.

I let Pru in, set the oven to preheat, and climbed up the stairs to my room to take a shower.

"Do we know the names of any of the people who live near here?" I asked the next morning at breakfast.

My father looked up from the newspaper. "I'm not sure anyone at all lives close by any more," he said thoughtfully. "Most of this side of town's been taken over by the developer—and, as far as I know, all the places nearby are either closed, or they've been demolished."

"It must have been pretty here years ago," Mom said. "All those lovely estates—it's a shame they had to go."

"But can you imagine trying to keep one up today?" said Dad. "Impossible to heat. Though most of them were just opened up in the summer—"

"—and the families moved back to the city in the fall," I said.

"That's right," said Dad. "It was a gracious way of

life and very pleasant for those who could afford it. Lots of help, maids and butlers—"

"And gardeners," I said.

"Lots of gardeners, too." Mom nodded. "They'd certainly be needed, with all those huge lawns."

"And miles of rose gardens, I suppose," I said.

Mom smiled. "Beautiful gardens. In fact, there's a particularly nice rose that was developed somewhere near here some years ago. It was a pink rose and the gardener named it after the place where he grew it."

"Babylon," I said without thinking.

Mom got up to pour another cup of coffee. "That's right," she said absently. "Imagine your knowing that— I'd forgotten all about it. It *was* called the Babylon rose. I tried to grow it myself one year, but the winters were too cold for it in Minnesota. I think I'll try it again now that we're going to live in the area where it grew originally."

She and Dad went on talking about gardens. I excused myself and started down the hill to feed Candy.

Roses. Who cared about roses? And especially, who cared what anybody called the silly things? Babylon. What a stupid name for a flower.

My sneakers squished through the dewy grass. It was going to be a beautiful day. I could hear Hilary's soft voice in my head. *How many miles to Babylon? Three score miles and ten*—I wondered how far a score of anything was. I'd have to look it up in the dictionary.

30

Can I get there by candlelight? Yes, and back again.
I dipped the scoop deep into the grain and fed
Candy her breakfast. As I waited for her to finish, I
leaned on the lower half of the stall door that led into
the paddock. Pru jumped up to sit on the door beside
my shoulder, fluffed out her thick coat, and began to
wash her face in the sunlight.

Late yesterday evening, when it had been dark and
I'd been tired, I'd promised myself I'd only ride in the
walled orchard and not try to go into the woods again.
But in the fresh new morning everything looked bright,
and I was curious—I wanted to go back to see Hilary
again.

I waited till afternoon. I had plenty of things to keep
me busy. I cleaned Candy's stall and dusted the last
few cobwebs from the window, and later I washed
Candy's tail and rinsed it in warm water I carried
down from the house. A judge had told me once at a
pony show that Candy's full white tail looked like a
bridal veil, and it did—it reached almost to the ground
and I took very good care of it. While it dried I
trimmed Candy's ears and fetlocks, groomed her, and
brushed out her mane.

Candy looked like a cake decoration made of spun
sugar when I was done. I was streaked with soapsuds
and dust from Candy's coat, and looked as though I'd
spent my life in a pigpen. Laughing, I went up to the

31

house for another shower and put on a fresh pair of jeans and a clean sleeveless shirt. I made myself a peanut butter sandwich, and as I drank a glass of milk I thought about the taste of Hilary's lemonade.

With a growing feeling of excitement, I fastened my hair back with a rubber band and went to get Candy.

I'd found a small can of oil in a toolbox. I'd even remembered to put it in my pocket. When we reached the narrow iron gate I jumped off Candy's back and knelt beside the rusty hinges. I squirted a thin stream of oil into the hinges, stood up to put some on the latch, and wiped my hands on a bunch of orchard grass. While I waited for the oil to work, I tucked the can under a bush and pushed back a few more honeysuckle vines and some ivy I'd missed the day before.

Candy jerked her reins impatiently. I gave the gate a yank. It swept open silently, nearly tripping me off my feet. I led Candy through into the woods, shut the gate, and flung myself up on her back.

Chapter Seven

I kept my reins short and one hand on Candy's mane after we'd crossed the stream. "No surprises," I said firmly to Candy. "You probably dumped me right on my head yesterday, not on my back. I probably made this whole thing up. The lawn, and the lake, and the gardens. And Hilary. Nobody like Hilary could be real."

Candy tossed her snaffle bit with a silvery chink and I let her walk on, around the last bend in the path and out into the bright sunlight on the lawn.

If all the big houses around here were deserted or torn down, why was I smelling the sweet, hot scent of freshly cut grass? There were the rose gardens, neatly kept, off to the left, and the lacy white summerhouse on the rise toward the right. Fall or no fall, they were just as I'd remembered them. Candy nickered softly. A dot of white was bouncing toward us like a ping-pong ball.

33

I shrugged my shoulders. "Nanette," I said softly. Candy nickered again—she wasn't afraid of dogs, she'd just been startled the day before when Nanette had rushed out at her, barking, without warning.

"Nanette!" I heard Hilary calling.

"Hi!" I said, urging Candy into a trot. "We're back!"

Hilary ran down the slope of the hill toward us with her skirts and petticoats billowing behind her. "I'm so glad to see you," she said breathlessly. "I was afraid you might not come."

I got off, slipped the reins over Candy's head, and held onto them tightly as we walked together toward the summerhouse. Nanette ran in circles around us in a flurry of snowy paws, white coat, and wagging tail.

"Do you think I might lead Candy?" Hilary asked shyly. I twisted the soft leather of the reins awkwardly in my hands.

"If she got away from you, I'm not sure how I'd ever get home," I said finally, not wanting to be rude, but suddenly nervous. I had awful visions of Candy disappearing again—if she went anywhere, I wanted to be sure I went with her.

"Of course," said Hilary politely. "I shouldn't have asked."

There was a brief but uncomfortable silence.

"Do you ride?" I said, groping clumsily for something—anything—to say.

Hilary smiled. "Oh, yes," she said. "Ever since I can remember. Father said I could have a new pony this summer, but my mother wasn't sure. And then they went off on their trip, and I suppose he forgot. And I know Madame told him it would make her nervous— she doesn't really believe that girls should ride at all, or have anything to do with horses. I don't think girls do much of anything fun where she comes from.

"I'm so bored this summer I could die, I really could." She swept her soft, wavy hair back from her face and forced a smile. "Madame also says I complain too much and that I must learn to accept life more gracefully."

"That's tough," I said feelingly. Hilary glanced at me with quick amusement.

"Tough. What a perfect word. Yes, it *is* tough doing practically nothing all day, every day. And the whole summer still ahead."

There was a pitcher of fresh lemonade waiting for us in the summerhouse, with several glasses on the tray.

"I told Cook that my cousins might be coming to see me today," said Hilary, "so she'd send down extra glasses and extra cakes. Of course my cousins are spending their summer in Saratoga this year, but Cook doesn't know that." She giggled and offered a small iced cake to Candy, who particularly liked the candied violet decorating the top.

"Now," said Hilary, "could I watch you ride? I didn't have the chance to see much of you on Candy yesterday."

"Sure." I was always glad to show Candy off. We

went down to the oval lawn between the rose gardens, by the lake, and Candy and I walked and trotted and cantered, and then did two nice figure eights.

"Lovely," said Hilary as I rode over to where she was standing near the rose bed. I glanced at the soft loam around the roses guiltily, but the deep hoofprints Candy had made the day before had been raked smooth.

Hilary noticed and shook her head. "I told you not to worry," she said. "The gardeners straightened everything up early this morning."

She picked a rose from the plant nearest her and tucked it into Candy's browband. "There," she said. "She's won first prize. Sorry it's only a pink rose, Candy. They don't come in blue."

Hilary took a step back with her hands clasped behind her back. "I wonder," she said shyly, "if you might let me ride her one day."

"Of course," I said with a quick smile. I didn't like anyone besides myself riding Candy, but the offer seemed perfectly safe. I didn't think for a minute that Hilary wanted to ride bareback, and I didn't even know where my saddle was—only that it was safe in a packing box somewhere, probably in storage with most of the furniture waiting to be unpacked in our new house in the fall. I seldom used it, anyway.

"Marvelous," said Hilary. "That's very kind."

We walked back toward the summerhouse.

"Did it take you long to learn to ride the way you do?" said Hilary as we sat down on the summerhouse steps. "I should think riding astride would be more difficult than riding sidesaddle."

"I don't know," I said slowly. "I've never ridden any other way."

"Really?" Hilary said in amazement. "But now that you've come to live in the East, won't you have to learn?"

"I hadn't thought about it much," I said. I got up to fuss unnecessarily with Candy's bridle and glanced sideways at Hilary.

Hilary was strange. Was that the right word? I wasn't sure. Unreal? No, she was real enough. I had wondered, as I'd ridden through the woods that afternoon, if maybe I might have made her up—perhaps I really had fallen on my head when Candy'd tossed me off the day before.

But as Hilary smiled and went over to pat Candy, I shrugged my shoulders. I knew very well I hadn't fallen on my head. It was my leg that was black and blue from where I'd hit the ground. And Hilary was wearing a different dress, pale yellow this time, with a dark yellow sash, and surely if I'd imagined all this, she wouldn't be wearing different clothes. . . .

"I'll teach you how to ride sidesaddle, if you'd like me to," Hilary said eagerly. "It would be fun. I have French lessons every morning, but I always come down here alone to the summerhouse in the afternoon." She giggled. "If I'm not doing needlework, Madame gives me books to read to improve my mind while I'm by myself. Have you read *Little Lives of Royal Girlhood?* That's what I'm supposed to be reading. Don't bother, it's dull. But I found a copy of *The Three Musketeers* in my brother's room, and I keep it hidden down here under the cushions. I've already read it twice."

She swung away from Candy with a swirl of skirts. "So you could ride over here in the afternoons, on Candy, and it can all be a secret—"

"I'd really like that," I said enthusiastically, It did sound like fun. "But I haven't got a sidesaddle—" I thought briefly of the old sidesaddle I'd found in the attic of the carriage house, but it was too dried out and old to be safe to use.

"We can use mine," said Hilary. Her eyes were shining and her face was flushed with excitement. "I'll smuggle it down here somehow. No one need ever know."

Chapter Eight

Hilary sat down again on the steps of the summerhouse and I sat on the lawn nearby to hold Candy while she nibbled at the grass.

"My own pony was just Candy's size," said Hilary. "Only he was black, with four white socks and a star. His name was Trinket. He got out of his stall one night late last summer and jumped into the vegetable garden —the gardeners found him in the morning. He'd eaten all kinds of things he shouldn't have, and almost all the corn."

Hilary's eyes filled with tears. "He was terribly sick. Mother wouldn't let me stay with him, but I climbed out the window and went to the stables every chance I could. I knew the grooms wouldn't tell on me. They did everything they could, but nothing helped— he died."

"I'm so sorry," I said awkwardly.

"I still miss him," said Hilary. She sniffed and pulled a handkerchief from her sleeve.

"Forgive me," she said. "I didn't mean to get all weepy. But with everybody away for the summer, and no pony to ride, and nobody to talk to except Madame —I guess I was feeling a little sorry for myself. But now you've come. You and Candy. It's marvelous. And we can have a wonderful time."

Sitting in the sunshine, we talked about her pony and Candy. Hilary relaxed with a little sigh and stretched her legs out, wiggling the toes of her high shoes. "They pinch," she said, "and they're hot. I wish I could wear little soft shoes like yours—I've never seen any quite like them before."

I stuck out my own toes and gazed fondly at the holes in my blue sneakers. "They are comfortable," I said. "But you could take your shoes off and go barefoot. For a little while. Don't you ever go barefoot on this beautiful lawn?"

"Barefoot." Hilary looked thoughtfully at her shoes. "I don't know why I never thought of that." She glanced over her shoulder toward the big house half-hidden in the trees and hesitated. "If Madame ever caught me going barefoot—"

She tugged at her shoe and tossed her hair back impatiently. "If I take these off, I'll never get them done up again. I haven't got a button hook with me."

I looked more closely at the row of tiny round buttons on the side of her shoe. "That's terrible," I said sympathetically. "It must take you forever to do those up every day."

"It does." Hilary sat back and clasped her arms around her knees, turning her face up to the sun. "Madame says I'm getting freckles because I forget to wear my hat. And she considers that a tragedy. She made me rub cucumber slices on my face last night before I went to bed."

We both laughed. Nanette rolled over on her back and went to sleep. Candy stood quietly, only moving her head and pricking her ears occasionally to watch the swans drifting slowly across the blue lake. Hilary and I sat in comfortable silence in the dreamy summer afternoon.

"I suppose I ought to go home." I got to my feet reluctantly.

"You'll come again tomorrow?" Hilary stood up and put a hand on Candy's reins.

"I will if I possibly can," I said.

"You know the way now," said Hilary. "I still don't understand exactly where you live, but it doesn't matter, does it? As long as you're close enough to come back."

"I don't know how far it is, either," I said as I got up on Candy. "But I'm sure it can't be as far as it is in the rhyme—three score miles and ten, whatever that is."

"It would be seventy miles," said Hilary with a smile. "I should imagine that part of the poem is more of a symbol than a reality."

"Sure," I said. I wasn't really listening. Candy was

fidgeting and I was having trouble holding her still. I'd forgotten to wear my watch, but I knew it was getting late. The warmth had suddenly gone from the sun and I shivered in my sleeveless shirt.

Hilary held onto Candy's reins for a moment longer, gave her one last pat of farewell, and then stood waving silently, with Nanette by her side, as I rode across the lawn, down to the path into the woods.

Candy jogged gently toward home. The light in the heavy woods shimmered and grew dim. The smell of crushed ferns and moss under Candy's hoofs swam up around us like mist.

I glanced back at the darkening woods and suddenly I shivered again. I patted Candy uncertainly on her shoulder. A faint flicker of doubt was making me uneasy. Who was Hilary, anyway? And what was she doing there, really, alone in the summerhouse, on the sunny lawns of Babylon?

"I'll bet," I said slowly to Candy, "that Hilary's nothing but a fake. I'll bet the whole set-up there is for a television commercial. For dog food or something. Or a cheap movie. I'll bet the cameramen were hidden right behind the summerhouse, laughing their heads off."

Candy paid no attention, of course, other than flicking her ears in a friendly manner at the sound of my voice, so I just nodded my head. I could imagine what was really going on, back where we'd just come from. Packing up all the props while Hilary put her hair up, changed out of her funny clothes, and drove back to New York to a party.

I felt more and more foolish as Candy picked her way through the stream and broke into a gentle canter. The little white summerhouse, the gardens, the lake with the swans, the long roofline of the big house just showing over the tops of faraway trees—fake. All of it.

I didn't like feeling I'd been made to look like a fool. I decided that Hilary had taken advantage of me, lonely as I was in a strange new part of the country. I wouldn't go back the next day, or ever again. For the second time I told myself that the orchard at home was a perfectly good place to ride; Candy and I would just stay where we belonged.

Candy stopped when we reached the gate. I got off. The pink rose Hilary had tucked into Candy's browband had wilted and lost most of its color. I pulled the limp flower from the bridle and tossed it as far as I could into the woods, then led Candy through the gate and kicked it shut behind us.

Chapter Nine

It poured rain the next day. Not just a soft, warm summer rain, which was marvelous to ride in, but a bucketing great lashing rain that kept Candy shut in her stall and me trapped inside the house.

I spent the morning curled up on the couch in the living room, with Pru purring by my side. I'd found my old scrapbook in a packing carton in my room and I turned through the fat pages, looking at snapshots of Candy from the day we'd first gotten her, and reading clippings from local papers about horse shows I'd ridden in.

My name was in some of the clippings, and one paper had a photograph of Candy winning a pleasure driving class. She was harnessed to a little metal cart with bicycle wheels and wearing a borrowed harness, and she'd behaved very well. She looked very pleased with herself and the ribbon on her bridle, and I looked as pleased as she did, sitting on the slippery narrow seat of the cart holding the silver trophy in my hand.

45

A lot of my friends' names were there in the clippings, too, and I wondered sadly if they missed me. We wrote letters to each other, of course, but it wasn't the same. I wondered what they were doing this summer, and whether they thought about me when they all went riding together. . . .

With the scrapbook open on my lap, and the rain beating wildly at the window, Pru and I both fell asleep.

The whole day was gray and dull, but the next morning was bright and sunny again. Candy danced out of her stall with her head between her knees and her tail in the air—the rainy day of rest had done us both good.

Right after lunch I put on her bridle, and instead of going into the orchard and through the small iron gate to Hilary's, I rode past our house and down the long driveway at a trot. I was determined to find the main entrance to Hilary's house. There was sure to be a mailbox or a sign on the road next to her driveway. It was time I found out about Hilary. She was a piece of a puzzle I couldn't quite fit together. If she was part of a movie or a television show, I'd be sure to find trucks and vans on the road or in her driveway. Maybe I'd even see actors I'd recognize.

We turned left at the end of the driveway, out onto the narrow paved road. The same towering wall of stone that separated our orchard from the woods ran along the road here, too.

It seemed I rode for hours. There was more traffic than I'd expected. I saw no cars or vans full of camera crews, but there were enormous, grinding dump trucks spilling dirt and stones out onto the road, and several motorcycles. Candy didn't like either the trucks or the motorcycles, and jumped into the ditch on the side of the road whenever one of them went by.

Candy was getting footsore. The paved road was hot and hard. I tried to ride on the grassy edge near the wall where the ground was soft, but then there were broken bottles to worry about, hidden in the grass and leaves. Finally Candy stepped into a plastic bottle carrier which stuck on her foot. I had an awful time getting it off again, and after I did, I gave up and went home.

"I wish I had a bicycle," I said suddenly at breakfast the next morning.

"You do?" Mom was astonished. "Since when?"

"Are you getting lonely, riding your pony every day by yourself?" asked my father. "I was afraid you might, living so far out of town, with no one your age nearby. How would you like to spend weekdays at the town swimming pool? It's over near our new house and I hear they've got a nice youth group—"

I could have kicked myself. I had only a few more

47

precious weeks of summer freedom, and I certainly didn't want to spend them in dreary organized games and projects with a lot of people I didn't even know. I'd have to face all that in the new school soon enough.

"No, thanks. Really," I said as quickly and firmly as I could. "I'm having a wonderful time. I just wanted to do a little exploring, that's all. Up the road and away from town, but Candy doesn't like the traffic."

"Let's have a look together, then," said my father. "I haven't had the chance to look around much, either. I'm sorry your mother and I have been so busy. But I've got a free morning—let's go in the car."

We turned left at the end of our driveway, as I'd done the day before on Candy.

We drove along in friendly silence. Dad was enjoying looking at the scenery; I never took my eyes off the unbroken line of the tall stone wall.

We turned left again at the crossroads. "Are you looking for something special?" asked my father.

"Not really," I said. I twisted my head to see over his shoulder. "Just wondering, I guess, where all those big old houses might have been."

"There were several out here," Dad said. "Sevenoaks—Greybriar—Hickory Hall—and I know that big wall to our left belonged to the estate they called Babylon. I asked the real estate agent yesterday because we'd been wondering about the Babylon rose. Remember?"

I nodded wordlessly. I remembered.

"There's nothing there now, though," said Dad. "It must have been a splendid place in its time. I hear there's even a lake—"

"Wow. Really." I slumped down in the car seat and let my hair swing forward to hide my hot cheeks.

"That's where the drive used to be." My father slowed the car. I sat up quickly. At last there was a gap in the high wall. Two square stone pillars marked the entrance to the drive. One of them held a single tall iron gate which was streaky with rust. The other matching gate was gone. Nothing but an overgrown track led out of sight through a weedy hollow where the driveway once had been. Five enormous boulders were placed across the opening and they obviously had not been moved for some time—untouched weeds grew over them and dead leaves were piled around them.

"No way to get a truck or a van in here, I guess," I said, trying to make my voice sound bored.

My father laughed. "Not through here, anyway," he said. "Just look at the size of the tree stumps on each side of the drive. What a shame all those beautiful old elms died. They must have been magnificent."

"They were," I said, remembering the sweep of the big trees which lined the drive up to the main house, behind the white roof of Hilary's summerhouse.

Dad looked surprised. "I've seen pictures," I said lamely. How could I tell him I'd been to Babylon on

49

Candy, that Babylon really was still there, in spite of what he'd been told and what we'd seen here by the huge old gate?

He'd be wild with worry, and he'd be sure to tell my mother. There'd be little visits to kindly doctors, and a swift membership in the swimming group—and certainly no more rides alone on Candy.

No, thank you. Much as I'd have liked to tell him about my visits to Hilary, if I said one word, I'd never see her again.

I didn't understand it all, not really. My mind was spinning with doubts and questions. I only knew that, in spite of it all, I'd enjoyed the afternoon with Hilary and I wanted to go back with Candy to Babylon again.

Chapter Ten

Hilary was waiting at the summerhouse for me that afternoon. I was a little bit late, because Mom and Dad were convinced I was lonely and had insisted I have a long, leisurely lunch with them before Dad left for still another trip to Boston. Mom was going out, too, something about looking at wallpaper samples, and tried to get me to go with her.

I was wild with impatience and nearly lost my temper, which would have caused all kinds of new problems. Mom finally said that I couldn't run around in blue jeans forever, that it was time I grew up and stopped being such a tomboy, and that she'd get flowered wallpaper for my room without me, whether I liked it or not.

I said I thought that was wonderful and even managed to smile as though I meant it, though I couldn't have cared less, one way or another, and finally I was free to get Candy.

We cantered most of the way through the woods. After I'd apologized to Hilary for being late and patted Nanette, Hilary said excitedly, "Let me hold Candy. I've got a wonderful surprise for you in the summerhouse." She took the pony's reins and I ran up the steps.

It was the first time I'd been inside the summerhouse. It was a six-sided room, with cushions on window seats along each side, and storage cabinets built under the seats. There was a woven round rug on the floor, and a low table that held a silver tray with the familiar cut-glass pitcher, filled with fresh lemonade, and a plate of cookies and cakes. Above the window seats the walls were open to the roof.

"What do you do if it rains?" I called back over my shoulder. "Doesn't everything get sopping wet?"

"The gardeners put everything away at night, or if there's a thunderstorm," said Hilary. "There's a lot of room in the cupboards." Her voice sounded impatient. "Look beside you, right near the door."

I turned and took a sudden, quick breath. Half-hidden in the shadow near the door was a small, glowing leather trunk with a curved top. The bright clasp on the front was an oval plate of gleaming brass, engraved with a clear, delicate pattern of leaves and flowers around the polished initials, HB.

I took a silent step back. "Can't you find it?" Hilary called breathlessly.

"I found it," I said, and my voice wobbled a little. Hilary was too excited to notice. "Open it," she said. I knelt on the floor of the summerhouse. I tried to make my mind a blank as I touched the shining clasp. But I knew exactly how to press it to make it open, without having to ask Hilary. The latch clicked and I lifted the curved lid of the trunk.

Everything was there, nested in fluffy layers of tissue paper. A small sidesaddle with graceful, curved horns—the leather of the stirrup and girths supple and gleaming, and the stirrup iron and buckles shining with polish. A long dark green skirt and a matching jacket were folded neatly in fresh layers of tissue, and there was a round green and black striped hat box at one side. I opened it and lifted out a small green felt hat with a red feather in its band.

"Say something!" Hilary said excitedly. "Do you like it?"

I got to my feet slowly, picked up the sidesaddle, and carried it to the doorway. "It's super," I said in a low voice.

"Super." Hilary repeated the word, as she always did when I used a word that seemed new to her. "Let's try the saddle on Candy. It should fit her well. I used it on Trinket, so it should be just the right size. I don't suppose, from what you've said, Candy's ever carried a sidesaddle before. I wonder if the balancing straps will bother her?"

"She's broken to harness," I said. "So she's used to the feeling of straps around her. She's pretty good about most things—I don't think she'll mind."

I carried the saddle down the steps and handed it to Hilary. "You'll have to put it on," I said. "I don't know how."

I took Candy's reins. Hilary's face was flushed with excitement and her gray eyes were sparkling. "This is such fun," she said. "When you didn't come yesterday, I was so afraid you might not come again."

All the questions I wanted to ask and all the doubts I'd felt no longer seemed important. They faded from the far edges of my mind like fragments of half-remembered dreams. I liked being here with Hilary. Nothing else mattered.

I held Candy as Hilary put the strange saddle on and fastened the girths. "Most of my friends couldn't saddle a pony if their lives depended on it," she said with pride. "Their grooms always do it for them. But Father believes that even a girl should know how to bridle and saddle her own pony."

She grinned over her shoulder. "Mother always said it was unladylike, of course. That a girl shouldn't be trained like a stable hand." She shook her head. "But Father insisted, and he taught me himself." She paused for a moment, with her hands on the saddle. "I only wish they'd let me do more."

She checked the tightness of the girths. "I haven't

54

made the back balancing strap very tight," she said. "Lead Candy around for a little so she can feel what it's like."

Candy didn't object to the new saddle at all. Hilary tightened the girths.

"Good," said Hilary. "Now you can get on."

"Me? Right now?" I stared at Hilary nervously. "On the sidesaddle? I don't know the first thing about it!"

"Oh, tush," said Hilary. "It's not difficult at all. Here. Let me show you." Before I knew what was happening, Hilary had gathered Candy's reins and, with a flurry of wide skirts, was up on the pony and in the saddle.

Candy blinked and turned her head to inspect the skirts brushing her side. But she'd been ridden in costume classes at pony shows, and I'd ridden her once to a Halloween party, dressed as a ghost, draped in long white sheets, so I knew she was just curious, not frightened.

Hilary tucked her left foot into the stirrup and smoothed her skirt. "Right," she said crisply. "Now, if you'd just hand me my crop—it's there, beside the steps."

"But Candy doesn't like crops," I said. Suddenly I felt desperately nervous. Suppose Hilary just rode off on Candy—would I ever see either of them again? And if Hilary took Candy away from me, would I ever be able to find my way home without her?

I stumbled around, looking for Hilary's crop while she and Candy waited patiently. Eventually I found it in the grass and handed it uncertainly to Hilary. "Candy's not used to crops," I said. "She doesn't like them waving around."

"I shan't be waving it around," Hilary said gently. "Riding sidesaddle, with both legs on one side, a good rider uses a crop as a signaling aide. Just as you use your right leg when you ride astride." She shortened

her reins, touched Candy lightly with the crop, and the pony moved forward at a walk.

Nanette sat companionably on the toe of my sneaker as Hilary rode away. Nanette wasn't worried, and I knew she'd never let Hilary out of her sight. I gave a shaky sigh and relaxed.

It was fun watching Hilary on Candy. Hilary was a very good rider, and after the first few minutes, Candy breezed along as though she'd carried a rider side-saddle every day of her life. She walked and trotted and cantered in smooth, wide circles on the lawn.

"She's lovely," said Hilary as she rode back to me. "Candy's perfectly, perfectly lovely. I hope you realize just how lucky you really are."

With a flourish of skirts she dismounted and stroked Candy gently on her shining neck. "It's easier in a proper habit, of course. Riding in a regular skirt bunches up the fabric and isn't very comfortable. Next time I'll wear my habit. That is, of course, if you'll let me ride Candy again."

"Of course," I said, pleased at how well Candy had gone and how much Hilary had liked her.

"Now, you try it," said Hilary.

Hilary held Candy while I climbed onto the strange saddle. I curled my right leg around the curved horn and put my left foot in the stirrup. I was terrified—it felt as though everything were going to tip over to one side.

"Don't worry so," said Hilary, trying not to laugh. "Let me just lead Candy a while so you can get used to it."

I started laughing myself after the first few anxious moments. Hilary was an understanding and patient teacher, always bright and smiling no matter how awkwardly I rode. We had a wonderful afternoon, and the time sped by so quickly that I had to rush to start home, though I stole a few extra minutes to rub the strange saddle marks from Candy's back before I left.

"Will I see you again tomorrow?" said Hilary.

"I'll try to come earlier—thank you!" I said, and waved. Candy broke into a canter as we turned onto the path through the woods.

Chapter Eleven

After the dishes were done that night, I mumbled something to Mom about making sure the latch on Candy's gate was tight. I found a flashlight that worked and, with Pru following at my heels and the blob of light from the flashlight bobbing in front of us, I went instead to the carriage house and squeezed through the sagging door.

The whole place felt thick with darkness. The huge main room with its musty smell echoed in a funny way, though I walked as quietly as I could, and my footsteps sounded like thunder to me as we crossed the harness room and started up the stairs.

I stood in the doorway of the attic room and swept the light across the floor toward the blank, dark window. The trunk with its curved lid was no longer there.

For one quick second my breath caught in my throat, then I shrugged my shoulders. Big deal. Builders and carpenters and men from the planning board had been on the place several times in the past few days. Any of them could have come up here. I moved the light quickly around the small room, but if anything else was missing, I couldn't really tell.

I sat cross-legged on the floor where the trunk had been and rested my head against the window. I switched off the flashlight and Pru jumped onto my lap. Together we watched the moon rise through the twisted branches of the apple orchard.

I tried to make my mind a blank. One of the pie-shaped panes of the round window was cracked, and I could hear the breeze whispering in the leaves of the big tree just outside. I listened, and thought about Hilary as I looked past the orchard to the high wall and the woods behind it. The little gate was deep in shadow, but beyond it the path must be brightening with moonlight, leading invitingly over to the wide lawns and gardens and the lacy white summerhouse—

I moved uneasily and clasped my arms around my knees.

Where did I really go when I rode over to Babylon? What really happened once I'd ridden through the narrow iron gate, under the arch of stone, on Candy?

Babylon was gone. Everyone said so—the real estate agents, and the surveyors, and the builders. I hadn't been able to find another way there, either, the day I'd looked out on the road, or the morning I'd gone out in the car with Dad. We'd found no entrance other than the unused driveway, shielded by the enormous stones that hadn't been moved for years.

I pictured Hilary lying in bed, listening to the night sounds the breeze made and watching the moon rise, just as I was. I tried to imagine what her room looked like, but I couldn't. Hilary would be looking forward to our next afternoon together with Candy. Tomorrow she'd be waiting by the summerhouse, wearing a dress no girl of my age had worn for almost a hundred years—

I put my hot forehead down on my knees. There. That was it. I had to admit to myself what I'd begun to believe. Hilary wasn't listening to the cars or the sound of the plane overhead, because in her world they didn't exist. They hadn't even been invented yet.

Ridiculous. I jumped to my feet and looked briskly for the flashlight. What I was thinking was impossible.

I found the flashlight and switched it on. "Come on, Pru," I said loudly. "It's time we went to bed." I snapped the attic door shut and hurried down the shadowy stairs.

But the next morning as I groomed Candy and cleaned her stall I wondered if maybe—just maybe—I was fooling around with something that was better left alone.

I stabbed the pitchfork into the manure cart and started to push it out of the stall. Candy, who was being really witchy that morning, blundered into the stall demanding an apple.

I didn't have one and I shoved her away crossly. She turned and bumped against the cart, which tipped and spilled all over the stall. I knew she'd done it on purpose. She and I glared at each other, she trotted merrily out into her paddock again, and I started to clean the stall for the second time.

I leaned on the pitchfork and brooded. Not about Candy, who was only being Candy, but about Hilary and Babylon. Either Hilary was strange, or I was getting to be.

I loaded up the cart again, shooing Candy firmly out of the way, and this time got it safely emptied.

On the way back to the stall I stood beside the paddock gate, staring into the woods. Maybe it would be better to slow things down a little. I decided I wouldn't go to Babylon that afternoon.

But I'd forgotten that Mom had invited a whole bunch of people for lunch. I saw their cars coming down the driveway. If I stayed home, I'd have to shower and change and run around all afternoon being polite to them while they chattered and fussed—

Quickly I put Candy's bridle on and hurried down to the gate.

"Keep your back straight!" Hilary said briskly. "And your chin up. Your shoulders must be square, just as though you were riding astride."

She put her head to one side and looked at me critically. "You really look nice in my habit," she said.

"I thought it might fit you well, since we seem to be just the same size."

I brushed a fleck of dust from the heavy green fabric that covered my legs. It had been Hilary's idea to have me try it on, and it was fun to learn how it fastened around my waist and how to manage it when I walked and rode. The short jacket with its velvet collar and cuffs fit me almost as well. It felt tight only if I let my shoulders droop, which I shouldn't do anyway. And when I pulled my hair back with a ribbon borrowed from Hilary, even her small green hat fit perfectly and stayed on no matter how uncertainly I rode.

Candy seemed to enjoy carrying the sidesaddle. I think she liked all the fuss. I could always tell when she was pleased with herself and having a good time. If she wasn't, she'd wear her ears at a cranky angle and switch her tail as she moved. But she was doing none of these things. She didn't even seem to mind my bumping around on the sidesaddle as I tried to learn how to post, though I had to admit she went even better for Hilary when it was her turn to ride.

"Try again," said Hilary. "You've almost got it right. Give Candy a little more rein, and for heaven's sake, keep your back straight!"

"Good!" said Hilary at last. "That was nice."

I pulled Candy to a stop, untangled myself from the saddle, and eased myself painfully to the ground. "I think you've ridden too long today," Hilary said sympathetically. "You're not used to this kind of riding. I should imagine your knees hurt from rubbing against the pommels—you don't want to get saddle sores."

I was afraid it was too late, but I didn't say so. I hadn't wanted to stop.

"You said you'd try jumping Candy today," I said quickly.

"I'd like to very much." Hilary's face glowed with pleasure. She swung herself lightly into the saddle, settled the skirt of her pink dress, and gathered Candy's reins.

We'd pulled a few fallen branches from the edge of the woods and made two inviting jumps on the lawn. Candy wasn't the least bit tired; she was fit, and still as fresh as a peppermint. I handed Hilary her crop and she and Candy cantered down toward the woods.

I ached with envy as I watched Hilary ride. Candy went like a feather for her, dropping her head prettily to the bit and flowing over the two jumps with an even, unbroken stride.

Hilary cantered back to me, smiling. "Would you like to try?" she said.

Trying to ignore my chafed knees, I climbed on Candy again. I thought I'd die of fright when we went over the first fence. Poor Candy—I yanked her terribly in the mouth as she jumped it, and then gave her an accidental whack with the crop over the second. At first I thought I'd fall off to the side in midair, and then I was sure I'd tip over backward. But eventually, after several more tries, Candy and I achieved a single decent jump and I pulled up triumphantly.

"That," Hilary said firmly, "was wonderful, but it's enough for one day. You really are going to be terribly sore if you're not careful."

I dismounted as gracefully as I could and led Candy back to the summerhouse.

We rested on the lawn on the shady side of the summerhouse, sipping lemonade and feeding Candy teacakes, which she'd come to expect and certainly deserved. It was very quiet. What little breeze there'd been had died, and hardly a leaf moved anywhere. From far away we heard a dog barking, and then a soft, murmuring jingle and the sound of hoofbeats of horses trotting gently and wheels turning on a graveled surface.

Far down the slope of the lawn, between the rows of huge elms that shaded the long drive leading toward the main house, an open carriage, drawn by a splendid matched pair of bay horses, moved into sight.

"That's Madame coming back from the village," Hilary said with an annoyed sigh. "I was hoping she'd stay out longer."

I didn't answer. Candy and I were watching the shining bays in stunned surprise.

They moved evenly along the drive between the trees with the bright sides of the open carriage and the brass buckles on the horses' harness winking in the sunlight. The horse nearest us turned his head a little and started to whinny to Candy. The coachman, tall and elegant in his top hat and dark green coat, touched the horse lightly on the shoulder with the whip. The horse straightened his head and settled back into stride with the horse at his side.

"You don't think they saw us?" I said frantically, jumping to my feet and turning Candy's head away in case she started to whinny in answer.

"Dawson probably did," said Hilary. "He's our coachman, and if anything distracts the horses while he's driving, he notices what it is."

I felt uneasy and got up to busy myself unnecessarily with Candy.

"He won't say anything, though," Hilary said reassuringly. "And Madame never saw us. She's hiding from the sun under her parasol. It's amazing she went out at all with the top of the carriage down."

"That's certainly a pretty sight," I said, half to myself, as the horses and carriage moved on at a dignified trot. I wished I could see them more closely.

Hilary nodded. "That's a nice pair, though Father and I prefer the chestnuts." She giggled. "They're a lot more fun to drive and they're a great deal faster, but Madame is like Mother. They don't like having the chestnuts out—they say they're too spirited to be quite proper."

Hilary reluctantly got to her feet. "I suppose it's getting late," she said, brushing the grass from her dress. We put everything away.

"I wish you could come have supper with us," said Hilary. "Perhaps, if we really tried, we could think of a way to manage it. But then you'd have to ride Candy home in the dark, wouldn't you? Isn't there any other way you could come?"

I stood with my hand on Candy's bridle. "There's no other way," I said. "I know, because I've tried."

Hilary frowned. "I don't really understand," she said at last. "But it doesn't matter, does it? Will you come tomorrow afternoon?"

I was up on Candy's back by then. "I will if I can move," I said through clenched teeth. "You're right. I've got such saddle sores—I can't believe it, after all the riding I've done."

Hilary shook her head in sympathy. "I was afraid we went on too long today," she said. "But you don't have to ride sidesaddle for a while. If you can ride at all tomorrow, please come—we'll find something else that's fun to do."

Smiling, she waved good-by as I turned Candy and made her walk quietly down the lawn to the woods.

Chapter Twelve

As things worked out, I couldn't go to Hilary's the next day, anyway. First Mom dragged me off to shop for clothes for the coming school year. Then we had to stop by the new house, which was almost finished. Of course, the builders had been saying that for weeks, but they seemed to mean it this time. I left Mom poking questioningly at a blueprint and talking to the plumber while I checked to make sure nothing had been forgotten for Candy's new stall, which was going to be added on to the back of the garage.

The stall was there, or the beginning of it was, and a pile of freshly cut post-and-rail fencing was heaped in the small field nearby.

By the time we finally got home, it was too late to go riding. Candy was perfectly content lazily grazing in her paddock. A day of rest certainly wouldn't have done her any harm, and I was still ferociously stiff and sore from all those hours in the sidesaddle the day before. I hoped I'd feel better by tomorrow.

But as I swung my legs out of bed and got cautiously to my feet the next morning, I knew it would be several days before I'd be able to bear getting onto a sidesaddle again.

When I rode back to Babylon that afternoon, Hilary was sitting on the steps of the summerhouse watching Nanette roll a red ball across the lawn with her paws.

When she saw me coming across the lawn on Candy, she jumped to her feet with a delighted smile. "Aren't you brave!" she said. "I wasn't a bit surprised when you didn't come yesterday—you really must be stiff. I should have stopped you much sooner than I did."

"I'm sorry." I slid gingerly off Candy's back. "I've spoiled our sidesaddle lesson."

"It doesn't matter," said Hilary. "I've had another marvelous idea. I had to think up a good excuse, so I told one of the stable lads I wanted to do some sketches this afternoon. Come see what I had brought down."

Leading Candy by the reins, I followed Hilary around the summerhouse. "Do you like it?" Hilary asked breathlessly.

I stopped so quickly that Candy walked right into me. While I sorted things out and hopped painfully on one foot, tugging my sneaker back over my heel which Candy had stepped on with the toe of her front hoof, I managed to say, "That's the prettiest cart I ever saw. Ever."

Hilary smiled and ran her hand along the gleaming shaft of a two-wheeled cart with delicate spindle sides.

It was painted deep green and black, with cream lines of thin striping on the spokes of each wheel and along each curved shaft. There was a small square door at the back with a bright brass latch, the cushions were cream-colored, and there were two pony-sized carriage lamps, each in its own round holder, on the shining sides of the cart.

"My father gave it to me for my birthday last year," said Hilary. "No one's ever driven it but me." She blew an invisible speck of dust from the bright finish on the side of the cart. "What do you think?" she said.

"I think it's beautiful," I said. I put my hands behind my back. It looked too pretty even to touch.

"Then I'll get the harness," said Hilary.

"Wait a minute!" I said with a gasp. "Hilary, you don't mean you're going to drive it with Candy—"

"Why not? Do you mind?" Hilary gave a skip of impatience. "You did say Candy was harness-broken. And my cart should be just the right size for her. Don't you think it would be fun?"

"Suppose something happens to it?" I said nervously. "Suppose Candy kicks it, or it gets scratched or something?"

"Pooh," Hilary said disgustedly. "How could it possibly get scratched, since all we'll do is drive it right here on the lawn? Anyway, it's only a pony cart, even if it is a particularly pretty one, and it's made to be used."

Hilary stopped and looked at me thoughtfully.

71

"Don't worry. I've had quite a lot of experience. Really. Father's even teaching me to drive the chestnuts. Though Mother doesn't know about *that*."

I shivered with excitement. I'd seen pictures of carts like this in books, but I'd never thought I'd have the chance to ride in one.

"Terrific," I said.

There was a woven wicker basket inside the cart. I helped Hilary lift it out. "This is my harness," said Hilary. "And if it fits Candy properly, then we'll know the cart's the right size for her, too."

We spread the glowing black harness out on the grass. It looked very much the same as the one I'd borrowed to use on Candy with the rickety metal cart in the past, though this one felt like glove leather in my hands.

"I hope you know how to harness up," Hilary said suddenly. "I never thought to ask. I've never been allowed to learn how."

I couldn't help smiling to myself. If Hilary's parents thought harnessing was unladylike, what would they think of my mucking out Candy's stall, and feeding and caring for her, all by myself?

"No problem," I said with more confidence than I really felt. I picked up the driving bridle and ran my fingers over the gleaming brass links across the brow band. They were polished so that they looked like gold, and matched the buckles and rings on the rest of the harness and Hilary's delicate monograms that shone on the blinkers and the sides of the harness pad.

Candy stood patiently as I slipped the driving bit into her mouth and buckled the soft round leather straps of the bridle in place. Hilary held her while I put the rest of the harness on, nervously looking for surprises. But there weren't any. All the girths and straps and traces went exactly where they seemed to belong.

While Hilary led Candy for a few minutes to get her used to the feel of a strange harness on her back, I went carefully over the brass and iron fittings on the cart.

It all seemed to make sense. I nodded wordlessly to Hilary, she held Candy still, and we ran the gleaming shafts through the loops in the harness.

"Don't let her move until I get everything done up!" I said to Hilary.

Hilary laughed. "I know better than that," she said. She patted Candy gently as I checked every buckle again, ran the reins through the rings, and buckled them to Candy's bit.

"Okay," I said.

"Okay," Hilary repeated with a smile.

I backed away from the pony and cart and stood looking at them, my heart pounding with happy excitement.

"What's the matter?" Hilary said anxiously. "Aren't you done *yet*?"

I'd seen carriages and carts in museums before, and always thought them beautiful. But I'd had no idea how different a really nice cart would look out in the open air with a live, pretty pony between the shafts. Everything twinkled and shimmered as Candy breathed or moved an impatient forefoot to paw at the grass.

I gave another shiver of delight and hurried to Candy's head. "You drive first," I said to Hilary.

With a quick flurry of skirts Hilary opened the little door at the back of the cart, called happily to Nanette to come sit beside her, and straightened the reins.

"I'm ready," she said. I got into the cart myself, fastened the door shut with a twist of its smooth brass handle, and nodded wordlessly to Hilary.

Chapter Thirteen

The cart, on its smooth springs and rubber tires, felt as though it were floating over the lawn. Candy jogged along gently, settling into the harness, and then Hilary sent her on into a stronger trot.

"Lovely," said Hilary. Candy raised her head, tossed the bit lightly, and swung cheerfully across the smooth grass. Every now and then she gave a discreet little skip of pleasure.

We spun through the golden afternoon. The few times I'd driven Candy, I'd clutched a rein in each hand—Hilary held both reins lightly in one hand and the delicate whip in the other, and the pony responded to her as though the reins were made of silk and the bit made of cobwebs. I sat perfectly still in silent admiration as Candy drew herself together, lengthened her stride, and swept in even circles and straight lines across the smooth grass.

"There. That was nice, Candy," Hilary said as she drew the pony back to a swinging walk.

I nodded speechlessly. I'd had no idea that my very

own pony, whom I thought I handled so well, could move with such grace in the hands of a skilled driver.

I finally said so as Hilary eased Candy into a more gentle walk to cool her out. This was hard for me to do, but I sighed and swallowed my pride.

Hilary smiled. "I know just how you must feel," she said. "Father takes lessons at the Coaching Club, and you should see what he can do with the chestnuts—and I think *I'm* doing well if I can have them going in stride together for more than a few minutes at a time! I'm certainly far from being an expert, but I can surely show you what I *do* know. It's such fun to share all this with a friend who really cares."

I settled back on the soft cushion with a wiggle of contentment and anticipation, as Candy walked lightly over the darkening grass.

The days and then the weeks of summer became a pattern of sunlit afternoons. Hilary and I took turns riding sidesaddle, or driving Candy on the wide, bright lawns of Babylon.

There were a few days, of course, when bad weather spoiled everything, or Mom suddenly would announce that she had other plans for me. Sometimes, too, I'd ride through the gate and the woods only to find the summerhouse empty, with no sign of Hilary or Nanette waiting to greet me.

I'd sit silently on Candy, both of us hushed and still with disappointment. This would always give me a quick cold, lost feeling and I'd gallop home to ride instead in the orchard near our house. But Hilary and I both understood we'd meet if we possibly could.

And then, suddenly, there were touches of gold and scarlet blurring the deep green of the trees. Faint traces of pale blue mist streaked the far edges of the lake and the woods. As Hilary was driving one afternoon, I was sitting dreamily on the opposite seat of the pony cart, holding Nanette on my lap.

"Hilary," I said, almost in a whisper, "this all has been so perfect. No matter what, this has been the most wonderful summer I've ever had."

"What a nice thing to say," said Hilary, pleased. "I'm sorry we've had to keep everything so secret, but Madame would never have allowed me to do any of this if she'd known."

"I understand. I really do," I said.

"But now the summer's almost over," said Hilary.

My stomach gave a sickening lurch. "I don't want to think about that," I interrupted quickly.

"But we must," said Hilary. "We must make plans. We've become good friends, haven't we?"

I nodded. "Then, you see," said Hilary with satisfaction, "we like to do the same kind of things and we have a good time together. Why should all of it end?"

I could think of a hundred reasons. Suddenly I felt a little bit afraid.

"Please, Hilary, let's not talk about it now," I said.

But Hilary wasn't listening to me. "Tomorrow's my birthday," she said. "And we always have a picnic on my birthday, if the weather's nice, on the far side of the lake. It's such a pretty drive, and you and I could go together in the pony cart with Candy. I've told Madame that I've invited you to come."

"*Hilary.*" My voice came out in a croak. "How can I possibly do that?" My hands felt sweaty and I rubbed them on my jeans.

My voice was starting to shake. "Listen to me," I said, and then I stopped. I couldn't think of the right things to say. "Let's not push our luck," I finally said lamely. "Why can't we keep things just the way they are?"

Hilary was quiet.

"Your coachman will recognize your cart and harness," I said, searching wildly for excuses. "Won't you get into trouble?"

Hilary shook her head. "Dawson will be pleased I've had a chance to drive it, in spite of them all," she said. "He'll not say anything in front of Madame."

I tried again. "I can't very well come in blue jeans and sneakers."

Hilary smiled. "Cowboy clothes might look a little strange to Madame," she admitted. "I'm afraid you'll have to wear a dress."

"I don't have the right kind," I said firmly. "Hilary, I can't begin to tell you how funny my dresses would look. Madame wouldn't approve. At all."

Hilary gave an impatient toss of her head. "That's nothing," she said. "You can wear the sidesaddle habit, then. Madame doesn't know it's mine, she's never seen me wear it. And it fits you well."

Hilary drew Candy back to a walk. "It's only for one afternoon," she said, "and you'll be home well before dark."

"I suppose it might work," I said finally. I was beginning to think of the idea with growing excitement. What harm could there be in going a little farther, and doing just this little bit more, with Candy and Hilary? Especially since we didn't have much more time together.

"We'll be moving soon," I said, feeling a sharp stab of sadness. "I'll be starting school, and you may be going to Switzerland—"

Hilary's hands tightened on the reins. "I won't go," she said flatly. "It would be like going to prison. No one seems to understand how I feel. And no one cares. I want to ride, and drive, and be outdoors, and do exciting and wonderful things. I want to learn to drive a pair really well, and even a four-in-hand one day." Suddenly she giggled. "Mother would faint if she heard me saying this, and so would my dreary friends. They're perfectly happy doing little nothings all day, and fussing about the silly knots in their embroidery—"

"Yuk," I said.

Hilary laughed out loud. "Yuk," she repeated. "What a splendid word. It sounds just like a cat being sick on the carpet."

She gave a light flourish of the whip. The tip of the lash floated out to flick a fly from Candy's shoulder.

"Nothing's really decided yet," Hilary went on eagerly. "Maybe you can come visit me in New York. You wouldn't have to go to school—you could have your lessons with me and Madame. We can ride together and drive Candy in Central Park, and my father will take the chestnuts out and let us come with him. And we can have sleighing parties when it snows—"

"Hilary," I said, almost in a groan. I wanted to stop her, but I didn't know how. It was all very well for me to think Hilary might be strange. But if I told her what was going on in *my* mind—

"You and me. And Candy, of course." Hilary drew Candy back to a walk with a quick nod of satisfaction. "Maybe I should capture Candy somehow, and then you'd *have* to stay with me."

She laughed and chirped to Candy, who swung into a bright trot. I sat for a few moments in thoughtful silence. I could be careful, and I wouldn't really have to say all that much, and I'd at least be able to see and share a little bit more of Babylon.

"Okay," I said. "Why not? Candy and I would love to come to your party."

Chapter Fourteen

I ran down the stairs that evening in a sudden panic. Mom was in the living room, making out still another list of things to do.

"I've got a problem," I said breathlessly.

Mom sighed. "I hope it's not a big one," she said with a tired smile. "All this planning and moving is driving me to distraction. But I'll help if I can. What is it?"

I stopped myself just in time. I realized that I could hardly explain to my mother that I needed a birthday present for Hilary.

"It's nothing, really," I said quickly. I sat down on the couch beside her. But Mom wouldn't be put off that easily, so I made up something about having lost my knee socks. "But I just remembered where I put them," I said lamely.

Mom looked at me suspiciously, then smiled and shook her head. "You exaggerate things so," she said with a laugh. "Or do you just make things sound more dramatic than they really are?" She gave me a hug.

I couldn't help wondering for a moment what her reaction would be if I tried to tell her about Hilary and where I went on my afternoon rides with Candy. "I'm sorry this summer's been so dull for you," Mom said absently, glancing at the papers in her hand. "Are you sure it was only your socks you wanted to ask me about? No other problems?"

"No other problems." I stood up, but Mom was already absorbed in her lists again, and I quietly left the room.

It took me a while before I finally thought of something I could give Hilary. I'd always given my friends records or tapes for their birthdays, but Hilary wasn't going to be that easy. I wandered around the house, got a carrot from the refrigerator, and went down to the paddock to talk it over with Candy.

It was a beautiful night, full of stars and warm breezes, and I'd latched Candy's door open so she could wander into her paddock if she wanted to.

Candy finished the carrot and begged for more. "You're spoiled," I said as I patted her soft muzzle. "You've had too many cakes and cookies all summer—"

This gave me the answer I needed. I ran back up to the house. My friends had always said I made the best tollhouse cookies they'd ever tasted, and I'd made batches and batches of them for every party we ever had. I'd do the same for Hilary.

The cookies came out well, but that was only the first part of the problem. I didn't want to carry them in a plastic freezer container. I wanted to use something prettier, but I couldn't find a nice box anywhere in the house—nothing but huge brown packing boxes, and they certainly wouldn't do.

I thought of the ideal solution, though I hesitated a few minutes before deciding to do it. Candy and I had won a small silver bowl at the 4-H horse and pony show last summer. Mom had taken it to the engraver, who'd put the word *Candlelight* on it in flowing script. It was the only really pretty thing I had that seemed just right for Hilary. I polished it tenderly—I hated to let it go, but I had to. It was perfect. I filled it with cookies, wrapped it in tissue paper, and tied it with a pale yellow ribbon I found in Mom's sewing box. It looked a little lumpy, but nice.

It was very late by then. The moon was already high. Pru had gotten tired of waiting and had gone up to curl up on my pillow. I hid Hilary's present in a bureau drawer and fell asleep the moment my head hit the pillow beside Pru.

Chapter Fifteen

Pru tried to follow us the next afternoon. I couldn't
believe it. She'd never tried to do such a thing before.
She followed Candy and me all the way down to the
gate in the orchard wall. I shouted and waved my arms
at her, but nothing I did made any difference, so I
finally had to get off, pick her up, and carry her back
up to the house.

The whole day had been a mix-up from the very
beginning. It had started out cloudy, and the weather
forecast predicted rain for the afternoon. I was almost
wild with disappointment, but the forecast was wrong,
after all, and the sun came out in a brilliant sky just
after eleven.

Mom had announced at breakfast that we were to
go shopping that morning for school shoes for me. I
said I couldn't possibly go that day—I simply had to
give Candy a bath. Mom could not understand why
Candy had to have a bath that very morning, and I
certainly couldn't tell her it was because I wanted to

have her looking particularly pretty for Hilary's birthday party in the afternoon.

Finally, after I'd promised almost hysterically to be available to go with her any other day but this, Mom threw her hands in the air and found something else that needed doing, and I was left to get Candy ready in peace.

I washed and brushed and trimmed her, and finished by combing her pale silver mane and tail until they flowed like silk. I put on her blue and white stable sheet to keep her clean, shut her up in the stall so she couldn't roll in the grass, and hurried up to the house to get ready myself.

Getting ready took longer than I'd planned because I couldn't find the shampoo when I started to wash my hair. Sopping wet, I finally found the bottle under a sweater in my room. Resolving, as I always did, to be more tidy in the future, I hurried as I washed my hair, and it tangled into knots.

I burst into tears of frustration. I was trying to comb my hair, find a clean shirt, and get into my jods, all at the same time. I struggled into my jodhpur breeches and short paddock boots because I thought they'd look better under the sidesaddle skirt than the jeans and frayed sneakers I usually wore to Hilary's. And then I had the laces of the boots to do up, which always took forever, even when things went right.

Eventually, though, everything got done. I even

remembered to take Hilary's present with me. After going back to shut Pru in the kitchen, Candy and I finally made it safely through the iron gate, into the soft green stillness of the woods.

Candy walked and jogged gently along the path. I rode with the reins in one hand and Hilary's present in the other. I breathed the sharp, clean scent of moss and ferns and listened to the soft sound of Candy's hoofbeats. In the welcoming quiet of the woods the little harried knots in my stomach slowly unwound, one by one.

Hilary was waiting with Nanette by the oak at the edge of the lawn. She was wearing a pink and white print dress with a taffeta sash and a matching wide ribbon tying her hair back in a bow.

"Happy birthday, Hilary," I said as I gave her the present.

"Thank you!" said Hilary breathlessly. "I was beginning to be afraid you might not be able to come!"

We harnessed Candy, then Hilary held her while I struggled into the dark green habit. Hilary had brought a narrow ribbon to tie back my hair and a short white scarf to tuck into the high collar of the jacket. I buttoned all the buttons right up to my neck, put on the small felt hat, and then tugged on the gloves that Hilary handed me at the last moment.

"Hilary, I can't breathe!" I said with a wail. "It's too many *clothes*. I don't know how you stand it!"

Hilary laughed. "You can't go on forever wearing the cowboy clothes you've worn all summer," she said. "Remember to pick up your skirt a little when you walk so you won't trip over it. You just haven't had enough practice."

The jacket was hot and the long skirt twisted in a snarl around my legs, but I managed to stumble over to hold Candy while Hilary got into the pony cart, called Nanette, and straightened the reins.

I checked the harness once more to make sure I hadn't left any crucial buckles undone, smoothed Candy's forelock under the glittering golden links of the browband, and stood back for one last admiring look. Candy cocked one hip and sighed with boredom as she waited in the shafts.

"Is everything all right?" Hilary said anxiously.

"Everything's perfect," I said happily. I got into the cart and latched the little square door behind me.

Candy moved out into a flowing trot. We spun past the rose gardens and across the lawn, and swung onto a smooth unpaved road.

"Are we going to meet the others up by the house?" I said eagerly. I was longing to drive past the main house, to see more of it than just the roofline over the trees. And I wanted to go by the stables. But Hilary shook her head.

"This is the first chance we've had to get away from

the summerhouse lawn—I want to take you for a real drive, just this once. We'll go on by ourselves. We'll meet the others later." Hilary tossed her hair back with a smile.

"Okay." I wiggled back comfortably on the cream-colored cushion. It was a perfect afternoon for a drive. All the early rain clouds had blown away and everything sparkled and twinkled—the buckles on Candy's harness, the bright brass and glittering paint on the cart, and the ripples on the lake as we caught glimpses of it through the trees.

Nanette was sitting on the seat beside me. I put my arm around her and half-closed my eyes. The soft harness whispered and the buckles and Candy's bit chimed softly. Her hoofs made crisp little sounds as she trotted on and the cart moved lightly and almost soundlessly behind her. I gave a sigh of pleasure and wished we could go on like this, through the shimmery golden afternoon, forever.

Woods and fields flowed past us. Hilary spoke softly to Candy and drew her back to a walk. "We're almost there," she said. "That was nice, wasn't it?"

I nodded dreamily. Hilary turned Candy neatly through an open gate between high hedges. More gardens blazed out toward the lake in front of us. Spidery white metal chairs and little round tables were set on the smooth lawn close by the shore of the lake.

"We're here first, after all," said Hilary. "But the

others will be along in a minute." She circled Candy and drew her to a halt beside the tall clipped hedge. As she was tucking the driving whip into the trim brass socket beside the seat, Candy raised her head and whinnied and a strange horse answered. There was the jingle of heavy harness and the sound of the hoof-beats of two big horses, trotting gently, in perfect stride together.

I gave a nervous gulp. "Help," I said. "I'd better get out. I have trouble enough with this skirt without strange people watching me." I fumbled my way out of the cart and somehow got safely to the ground, gave the skirt a quick kick to settle it in place, and hurried to Candy's head.

I could hear Hilary giggling behind me as she and Nanette followed. Candy shied as the big bay horses swung through the gate, pulling the open carriage which was full of maids and footmen and hampers. Candy snorted and blew and jumped up and down a little between the shafts, but she quieted as soon as the carriage turned and stopped.

The coachman touched the brim of his top hat and I saw him wink solemnly at Hilary. She nodded and smiled back as a footman in matching dark green livery went to stand at the heads of the gleaming bay horses. Another came to hold Candy. She blinked at him in astonishment. Not for the first time I wished I could ask her what she thought of all this—certainly it was all as new to her as it was to me. But Candy seemed to be enjoying all the fuss and formality.

I gave the footman an uncertain smile, patted Candy reassuringly on her silvery neck, and turned to follow Hilary.

"Madame," I heard her murmur. "I'd like you to meet my friend, Gail Simmons—"

Through all the summer I'd pictured Madame as tall and thin and ugly, with a mean face and dark little eyes. She wasn't that way at all. She was plump and sweet and looked much more anxious than bad-tempered, and instead of the stiff black dress I'd been sure she'd be wearing, her dress was pale lavender with a matching parasol.

I felt my face go scarlet as I fumbled my way through a curtsy I half-remembered from a dancing class at school years and years ago. I didn't know whether to offer to shake hands or not. I decided not, and whispered an awkward "How do you do."

Madame smiled. "How nice. Miss Simmons. Your coming has made a happy day for Hilary."

I managed a feeble smile back. Madame turned to Hilary.

"Hilary, my dear," she said, "you have forgotten your hat. *And* your gloves. Your parents will wonder what care I have been taking of you."

"I'm sorry," said Hilary, not sounding sorry at all.

"They are in the carriage," said Madame.

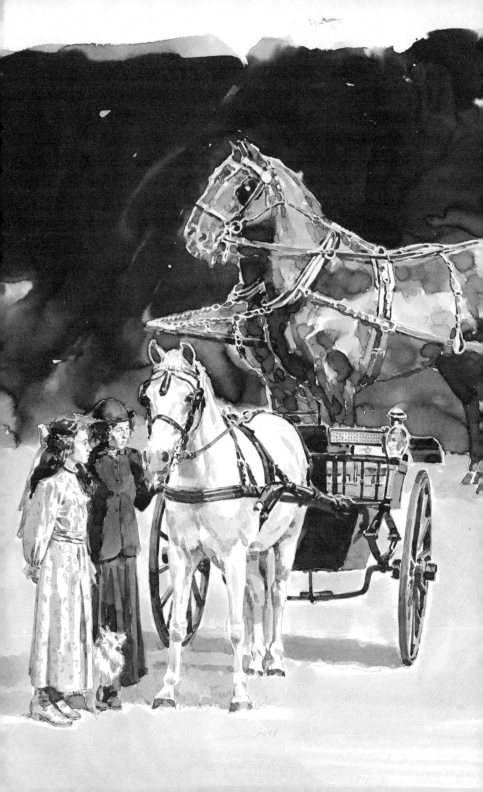

"Bother," said Hilary under her breath. I went with her back to the carriage and stood admiring the glossy bay horses, trying to understand how all their harness went together, while Hilary found her wide-brimmed straw hat and jammed it onto the back of her head. Her hair ribbon slipped out of her hair. With a mutter of exasperation, she picked it up and shoved it into the pocket of her dress.

She shook out her skirt, put on a smile, and we went over to the grassy shore of the lake where Madame was feeding bread to the swans while Nanette watched, bouncing at the edge of the water.

We laughed and threw sticks for Nanette to catch while the maids in their full dresses and white aprons dipped and swooped like swallows, the ribbons on their white ruffled caps flying behind them. Embroidered cloths were spread on the tables. There were trays and plates of sandwiches and cakes, and a cut-glass punch bowl filled with raspberry punch, and round little punch cups with thin handles to drink from, and a cake for Hilary piled with white frosting and decorated with perfect little sugar roses.

Chapter Sixteen

Madame was laughing with us, and the party was a great success. Everyone had a piece of cake—including the coachman and the footmen and the maids—and the dignified coach horses and Candy each had one of the sugar roses from the cake.

Madame gave Hilary a heart-shaped locket. As Hilary thanked her, I remembered the present I'd brought—Candy's silver bowl of tollhouse cookies was still in the pony cart. But before I could go to get it, Madame handed Hilary a blue envelope.

"From your mother," she said. "It came just this afternoon, as we were leaving the house. I thought perhaps it was for your birthday, so I brought it to you here."

Hilary opened the letter with a smile. Slowly her smile faded, her gray eyes widened, and all the color drained from her face.

"She wishes me a happy birthday," Hilary whispered, "and then goes on to tell me that everything's been arranged. I am to go to boarding school in Switzerland."

Hilary jumped to her feet. She crumpled the letter and threw it to the ground. "I won't go," she said harshly. "I don't want to go to boarding school *anywhere*. I won't be shut up indoors—I don't want to study French verbs all day, and embroider, and do dull nothings for the rest of my life."

She turned and walked slowly away from the table with Nanette trotting soberly by her side. She stopped once and looked back at me, her face suddenly bright with hope. "Maybe you could come with me," she said. "I wouldn't be nearly as lonely anywhere if I had a friend who shared the things I like to do."

She put her hand out, reaching toward me. For one dizzy moment we looked at each other in shared understanding. I knew, just then, I could go with Hilary. Somehow, with no questions or complications, I could become part of her world—all I had to do was reach out and take her hand.

"Come with me," Hilary said again, gently.

Dimly I became aware of Candy moving uneasily between the shafts of the pony cart and I heard the muffled tap of her hoof as she pawed the short grass.

I looked down at my hands, which were clenched in my lap, pressed against the dark green fabric of the sidesaddle skirt.

I looked up again slowly. "I want to. I really want to. But you know I can't, Hilary," I said in a whisper. I started to stand up, but Madame took my arm. "Wait," she said softly. "Let her become—how shall I say it?—more tranquil of spirit for a moment or two."

I sat miserably still. I was more worried about Hilary than Madame seemed to be. I supposed, in some ways, I knew her better.

There was silence everywhere. Even the big carriage horses had stopped chinking their bits. The maids stood frozen beside the carriage where they'd been packing things away; one of them held a picnic hamper in her hands.

It was getting dark. Twilight had seeped into the woods and out onto the picnic grounds without my having noticed. The lake was still, as unmoving as a puddle of silver, and the swans were gone. The carriage lamps had just been lit on the big carriage and on the pony cart. They made pale white circles of light on the grass.

Hilary suddenly broke into a run. With a blur of whirling skirts she jumped into the pony cart. She called to Nanette and the little dog bounced in beside her. Without even pausing to shut the door of the cart, Hilary snatched the whip from the socket and brought it down, with a whistling slash, on Candy's back.

The stable lad standing, half-asleep, at Candy's head could do no more than try to jump out of the way.

Even so, I think the tip of the shaft caught him on his side, because he was rolling on the ground, clutching his ribs, as Candy bolted into a wild gallop through the open gates and swung out onto the road.

Two men were hanging on the heads of the bay horses, trying to control them as they reared and plunged in fright. The maids ran shrieking out of the way as the big carriage rocked and swayed and threatened to turn over. Madame stood up so quickly that her chair tipped over behind her. She grabbed at the table to keep her balance, so she had to take her hand off my arm and I was free.

"Candy! Hilary!" I was screaming as I tried to run, stumbling over the thick folds of the sidesaddle skirt.

I tore at the buttons that held it. Finally something gave and it fell away. I struggled out of the jacket without stopping, threw it to one side, and then pulled the white scarf from my neck. It dropped from my hand. It was easier to breathe now as I ran, and I was gratefully aware of the cool evening air on my bare arms and neck. I snatched the small felt hat from my head and sent it spinning wildly into the bushes at the side of the road.

I was terrified for Candy, and for Hilary, and myself. I'd been playing a game with rules I didn't know. I'd been smart enough to warn Hilary that we shouldn't try to push our luck too far, but not smart enough to follow my own advice.

I was sobbing for breath as I ran down the darkening road. The nursery rhyme Hilary had recited the first time we'd met kept time now with my running footsteps:

> *How many miles to Babylon?*
> *Three score miles and ten.*
> *Can I get there by candlelight?*
> *Yes, and back again.*

I'd made it to Babylon and back so many times that summer, and it had been so easy, but only on Candy— I'd not been able to get there any other way. Now I didn't know where Candy was, or where Hilary might go with her. And I was certain that unless Candy and I were together, neither of us would be able to get home from Babylon again.

I could hear the echo of Hilary's voice in my mind, "Maybe I should capture Candy somehow, and then you'd have to stay with me—"

"Hilary! Candy!" I tried to call out, but my voice came out in no more than a whisper.

I had to slow to a walk. My breath was rasping in my throat. My side hurt and it was agony to breathe. I bent over and then sank to the ground. It was useless to try to follow them any longer—Candy'd been running much too fast for me ever to catch up.

Dimly I heard the sound of turning wheels and of galloping unshod hoofs. But the sound was drawing closer, not fading away. I scrambled to my feet and pushed through the bushes at the side of the road, trying to find the direction the sound was coming from.

The bushes ended abruptly on the shore of the lake and I found myself standing where a narrow stream ran from the lake toward the arch of a small wooden bridge. The roadway had turned away from the lake toward the bridge—if I crossed the stream here by the lake, and ran fast enough, I might get back to the road ahead of Hilary.

The stream was shallow. I splashed through it quickly and forced my shaking legs into a stumbling run again up the bank toward the road.

But there wasn't time enough. I stood helplessly near the road as Candy came racing across the bridge toward me, with her mane and tail flying. She galloped past, so close that a spray of pebbles thrown back by her hoofs stung my face and bare arms.

Hilary's wide-brimmed straw hat was blowing to one side and her long hair whipped around her face. She was trying frantically to push her hair away from her eyes with one hand. Her other hand was unsteady on the reins.

Candy was tiring and running unevenly. She swerved, just a little. The wheel of the cart struck a stone or the tip of a fallen branch hidden in the grass near the road. There was a sharp crack as the axle snapped and the pony and cart went down.

Hilary was thrown out onto the grass. Nanette was hurled into a clump of bushes. I saw the little dog jump up, shake herself, and limp over to Hilary's side. But neither Hilary nor Candy moved. I ran and flung myself to my knees in the grass beside Hilary. Her eyes were closed but she looked as though she might be smiling. I tried to remember what little I knew about first aid. I loosened the top buttons of her dress, forcing the little round buttons through their tight loops, but I couldn't be sure she was breathing.

I knelt there helplessly, simply not knowing what to do. Then I heard, through the gathering darkness, the harsh jangle of harness and the rumble of wheels and the hoofbeats of horses being driven too fast—the big carriage was following after Hilary and would be here soon.

I ran over to Candy. She'd been lying so still that I was sure at first her neck had been broken, but then I heard her grinding her teeth with rage. She was tangled in the harness still buckled to the broken cart and couldn't get to her feet.

Candy moaned and ground her teeth again. Scared as I was, I had to choke back a giggle. "Cut it out, Candy. If you're that mad you must be all right," I whispered. In the pale pools of light from the carriage lamps I found what buckles I could, undid them, and pulled the harness away from the fallen pony.

I put my belt around her neck and took off the heavy driving bridle. Candy blinked up at me. "Get up," I said urgently, and gave the belt a tug.

Candy raised her head, then surged to her feet so quickly I nearly let go of her. She shook herself like a dog and then I led her forward a few steps. My knees sagged with relief—she was stiff and sore, but she could walk. Nothing seemed to be broken.

The sound of heavy hoofs and wheels was getting louder. Holding tightly onto Candy with one hand, I lifted one of the carriage lamps from its bracket on the side of the pony cart and went over to Hilary. Nanette, who was huddled close against her, whimpered and held up one paw.

Hilary hadn't moved. I propped the glowing lamp against a nearby bush and brushed Hilary's hair back from her cheek. Her face felt still and cool to my hand, but this could have been only because the breeze had gotten colder—it was blowing strongly now and ruffled her petticoats and the ribbon on the broadbrimmed hat that was lying on the grass beside her.

I stood up uncertainly. I wanted to stay until help came for her. I wanted to know if she was going to be all right—

Nanette whimpered again. I longed to pick her up to comfort her. More than anything, I wanted to take her home with me.

"You be good, Nanette, and stay with Hilary," I whispered to the little dog. "I don't think I'll ever be

able to come back again. You're the only friend she's got left."

I hesitated, but I could hear the hoofbeats of the horses growing louder. I knew the coachman would soon be able to see the broken pony cart on the road with its single lamp still burning, and the other lamp shining beside Hilary—

I wanted to call out to them, but my voice stuck in my throat. I felt somehow that even if I did call, no one would hear me, and no one would answer. Not any more.

I looked around wildly. Candy gave me a hard nudge with her muzzle. Tugging the pony behind me, I hurried over to the cart and reached under the cushion. Hazily I was aware, through all my grief and fear, that I didn't want to leave anything behind. Maybe if nothing of mine was there at Babylon, it would be as though Candy and I had never been there at all, as though none of this had happened.

I felt the hard edge of Candy's silver bowl where I'd tucked it under the cushion strap. I grabbed it with a shiver of thankfulness, struggled somehow up onto Candy's back, and kicked her into a gallop.

I clutched Candy's mane and the belt around her neck with one hand and held the tissue-wrapped bowl with the other. I glanced back, just once, and caught one last sharp twinkle of lights on the road before Candy swept around a bend and the trees blocked them from sight.

I didn't know where we were, but I'd been lost out riding before, and I'd always let Candy find the way home. She skimmed along the dark road and I sat as still as I could so she'd know I wasn't trying to guide her. The sky lightened as we came out of the woods and I recognized the silhouette of the summerhouse. against the stars.

Candy dropped back to a trot and whirled into the woods again, and I gave a shudder of relief as I heard the familiar sound of the mossy path under her hoofs and felt ferns brushing aganst my legs. Candy had found the path, and soon I heard the soft rushing of the stream we always crossed on our way home from Babylon.

It was desperately dark in the woods. Candy slowed to a walk. Only tiny slivers of reflected starlight splintered on the water as Candy picked her way carefully through the stream.

The ripple of the stream faded behind us. Night creatures rustled in the bushes beside the path and an owl hooted nearby. I'd always liked the sound of owls, and this one sounded particularly friendly in the darkness. I drew a breath so deep I could feel it practically down to my toes.

The woods began to brighten. The moon was rising. It was well up over the tops of the apple trees as Candy stopped beside the gate at the orchard wall.

Chapter Seventeen

Candy stood with her head over the stall door, looking down toward the orchard wall as I rubbed the harness stains from her coat. I was so tired and confused that I felt numb all over. Enough pale moonlight came through the upper door for me to see well enough as I comforted myself with familiar tasks—fresh water for Candy, and hay, and a whole heap of fresh shavings for her stall. I rubbed her legs and wrapped them in soft cotton and bandages and buckled her stable sheet snugly around her. I went to get a kettle of hot water from the kitchen and made her a steaming bran mash full of carrots.

The night was soft and silvery, but the breeze had changed to a funny little wind, which had started to blow in fitful gusts. It smelled and felt like rain. I shut the top door to Candy's stall and left her nibbling slowly at her mash. Pru was sitting on top of the fence post by the gate. I picked her up and buried my face in her heavy coat for a moment, then let her jump down from my arms. Carrying the teakettle in my hand, I made my way slowly back to the house.

Mom had gone to meet Dad at the airport. I blinked at the note propped against the sugar bowl on the kitchen table, glad I didn't have to try to explain why I was so late getting home.

I wasn't hungry. I floated in a hot bath until I thought I'd melt away, and it wasn't until I had gotten into bed that I felt the tug of the ribbon still in my hair. I pushed myself deeper into the pillows and untied the ribbon, pulling it gently through my fingers to smooth out the wrinkles. With the narrow green ribbon in my hand and the bedside lamp still on, I fell asleep.

It rained all the next day—a gray, dull rain that felt like autumn. I told my mother I felt sick, which I did, and except for struggling down to the stable in a flapping raincoat to care for Candy, I stayed in my room most of the day.

I had a miserable headache. I read for a while, and watched television until my mind went soggy, and the dreary day finally ended.

It was cool and bright and sunny the next morning. I wished I still felt numb and sick, but I didn't. After breakfast I turned Candy out into her paddock and for a while I watched her grazing in the sodden grass. She looked fresh and unruffled, completely content in her own pony way to search for the last sweet clover of summer.

I sighed and turned away. I called to Pru to keep me company. I'd go back to the attic room in the carriage house, I decided, and somehow try to make sense out of everything that had happened.

The door at the top of the stairs had warped a little. I had to jerk at it to get it open. Pru ran on into the dusty room ahead of me and I stood there, staring, as she jumped up onto the curved lid of the small trunk standing under the window.

I went over slowly, lifted Pru off, and pulled the trunk around so the light from the window fell on the faded, cracked leather and the dull brass trim.

I pressed the spring on the latch and it clicked open. Everything was there—the dried-out saddle and the faded green habit. Even the little green hat was there, though it was no longer in its round striped box. It was on top of the folded habit, and the red feather was broken. When I touched it gently, it crumbled into dust.

I closed the lid softly. My hand left bright streaks as I pressed the clasp shut. I rubbed the faint tracings of leaves with the sleeve of my sweater and the delicate engraving brightened. I could read the initials clearly for the first time: HB.

Hilary Blake. I sat back on my heels with my hands on my knees. Pru immediately jumped onto the trunk again. I got to my feet uncertainly and stumbled down the stairs.

Pru wouldn't follow me into the dim high main room of the carriage house. She didn't like the feel of the cold brick floor under her feet. I went alone to the broken pony cart, standing in the shadows at the back corner, caked with dust, tilted crookedly to one side.

Cobwebs were draped heavily over the wheels and I could see pale, ragged outlines of holes in the stained cushions where mice had made their nests, undisturbed for years. I touched the bent hinges of the square door at the back, then shrugged my shoulders and turned away.

I glanced over my shoulder. In spite of the shadows, the morning light was changing in the high windows, and I could see one small carriage lamp snug in its bracket on the side of the cart, its thick glass cracked and dull. Inside it was the stump of a burned-out candle.

The lamp on the left was gone.

I whirled and ran down to Candy's paddock. I searched wildly for her bridle in the stable and then out on the fence posts near the paddock gate, but I couldn't find it anywhere.

I stood still for a moment, gasping for breath. Candy lifted her head with her silver forelock blowing back against her pricked ears, and I remembered. Her bridle was lying by the steps of the summerhouse where I'd left it when I'd harnessed Candy to the pony cart on that last golden afternoon at Babylon.

It had been real. All of it had been real. I no longer cared whether it made any sense. Hilary had been hurt. I had to know how she was. I had to get back to Babylon.

I snatched Candy's halter and a lead rope from the stable and ran across the wet grass to her. She waited for me, though I had no treat to give her. I buckled the halter on with shaking fingers and jumped onto her back.

We galloped across the paddock, into the orchard, and down to the high orchard wall. I flung myself off while Candy was still moving and grabbed the narrow iron gate to keep my balance. I turned my hands over and looked at them, stunned. My palms were streaked with rust.

Honeysuckle and ivy were woven thickly through the gate. The latch was solid with rust—it looked as though it hadn't been opened for years. I searched frantically in the thick bushes beside the gate—the little can of oil was still there. I jerked the cap off but only a last few silky drops of oil dripped onto the latch. I put the can down in despair.

Pru came through the rough grass of the paddock and slipped silently into the tumbled honeysuckle vines. I stood with my hands on the gate, with Candy beside me, and looked across to the path curving out of sight into the deep, flickering shadows of the woods. I could imagine Hilary getting ready for the afternoon, putting her French books away, hurrying eagerly down to the bright white summerhouse with Nanette dancing beside her.

I could hear her soft voice apologizing for her behavior at the picnic, saying she was sorry her pretty cart had been broken, glad that Candy hadn't been hurt. It had been the fault of the wide-brimmed hat and her hair blowing over her eyes. The cart would soon be mended, we could go on with our sidesaddle lessons, and I could teach her, as I'd promised, how to ride astride—

I shook the gate until my hands stung, but it wouldn't move. Candy pushed it with her muzzle, and then raised her head and whinnied.

The sun was high. It was early afternoon. I could smell the cidery apples that had fallen from the orchard trees, and the heavy perfume of the last few blossoms on the honeysuckle vines. There was no sound except for the buzzing of a single bee. The last of the wind had died, and the leaves on the trees were still.

Candy whinnied again, almost desperately. This time the silence in the woods toward Babylon was broken by a strange new sound. Candy shied and pulled back. I listened, and then turned away.

Pru came over to press herself nervously against my leg. I put my hand on Candy's mane. From far across the high orchard wall, beyond the heavy trees, I heard the ringing sound of an ax and the deep snarl of a bulldozer. And I knew that Babylon was gone.

About the Author

Jean Slaughter Doty is the author of a number of fine novels popular with young animal-lovers. Among these are *Summer Pony*, *Winter Pony*, *Gabriel* and *The Monday Horses*. Under the name Jean Slaughter she also has written *Pony Care*, *Horsemanship for Beginners* and *Horses Round the World*, and compiled *And It Came to Pass*, which tells the Nativity story through Christmas carols. In addition, she and her husband, cartoonist Roy Doty, are co-creators of the annual *Macmillan Children's Calendar*. She and her husband, their children and various horses, dogs and Siamese cats live in West Redding, Connecticut.

F   Doty, Jean Slaughter

Can I get there by
candlelight?

DATE			
NO 26'80 FE 17'83			
AP 7 '82			
MR 9 '83			
NOV 21 1986			
NOV 30 1988			
OCT 5 1993 17			
DEC 18 '00 27			